Besides the Wench
Is Dead

By Margaret Erskine

MARGARET ERSKINE

Besides the Wench Is Dead

Published for the Crime Club by

Doubleday & Company, Inc.

Garden City, New York

1973

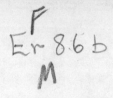

All of the characters in this book are fictitious, and any resemblance to actual persons, living or dead, is purely coincidental.

ISBN: 0-385-00435-4
Library of Congress Catalog Card Number 72–97090
Copyright © 1973 by Margaret Wetherby Williams
All Rights Reserved
PRINTED IN THE UNITED STATES OF AMERICA
FIRST EDITION

Besides the Wench
Is Dead

ONE

If it had not been for the articles in the *Daily Record* none of it would have happened. The undefended case of Harker versus Harker would have passed and been forgotten.

The highly photogenic Delia Sumner would have been seen arriving or departing from the court. The remarks of Mr. Justice Grant would have been reported. It would all have made very little impression on the general public.

As it was the sales of the *Daily Record* had rocketed. Delia Sumner, whose face and figure had been known chiefly to the readers of the glossy magazines, became more familiar than Miss World. She could not go anywhere without being recognised. She did not care. And, at the moment, her flatmate, Antonia Hughes, although unhappily aware of the interest they had aroused in the other people in the restaurant, had more important matters on her mind.

"I do hope you'll be all right, Dee," she said anxiously.

"Of course I shall." Dee flashed her companion an amused glance. "Always remembering that in every man in sheep's clothing there is a wolf struggling to get out."

"You'd be safer if you just remember that behind every married man there is a wife ready to spring out," said Antonia dryly.

Dee's good-natured face screwed up in a grimace. "I admit that being corespondent in a divorce case hasn't done my career any good. Obviously it's untrue that any publicity is good publicity."

"Dee, you know it wasn't the divorce case. It was those interviews you gave to the reporter on the staff of that wretched rag."

"Well, he was awfully dishy. A real sweetie."

Antonia sighed. "Sometimes, I think it's a pity you have a private income. If you hadn't, you might take your career more seriously."

Dee shook her head. "I wouldn't, you know. I was born a marauder. I enjoy sex and that's all there is to it." She added: "And anyway I don't know what you're complaining about. The divorce case is over. The newspaper articles have come and gone. True, at the moment, I'm not in demand as a model but if I were I wouldn't be able to spend a fortnight at Hone and you'd be alone for much of your holiday." She returned to her meal with undiminished appetite.

"I just wish Mrs. Harker didn't live there."

Dee grinned. "If the Harkers hadn't had a house at Hone I'd never have met their Maserati—and boy, was she a beauty?"

"Things could be unpleasant," Antonia persisted.

"You're thinking of George? I admit he's been a bit of a nuisance but he must have given up by now."

"It's not George Harker. It's his wife I'm thinking about."

Dee looked surprised. "But she was the one who brought the divorce suit. And she did know that I didn't want George for keeps."

Said Antonia slowly, "I think Mrs. Harker would feel that made it worse. After all, they had been married for nearly twenty years."

"But she broke it up—and for what? I was only in love with the car." Dee's cheerful, unrepentant grin lit up her rather broad face. "Sounds kinky, doesn't it?" When she saw that Antonia still looked anxious she added: "Honestly I don't think you need worry. The Harkers don't count for much in Hone. They only bought the Limes three years ago and that isn't long enough even today."

Antonia was silent while an attentive waiter removed their plates and brought coffee. For some time now she had been aware of a vague feeling of disquiet. Of a face half seen, a glimpse of a tall ramrod-stiff figure, of dark glittering eyes full of hatred—

"Dee, listen," she said as soon as they were alone again. "Several times since those wretched articles appeared, when we've been together, I've thought that I've seen Mrs. Harker following us either on foot or in the car. This morning, as you know, I went out early to get the coffee you'd forgotten to buy. When I turned into Belton Street there was her white Ford Anglia parked where she could watch our block of flats. And she was sitting behind the wheel quite still, staring at the entrance."

"Dark hair, stony face and all," Dee ended with a grin. She was shaken but more puzzled than anything else. "It's a bit off-putting to think she's following me about. What do you think she wants?"

"I wish I knew. I spoke to Dennis"—this was one of the porters and an admirer of Dee's—"about it. He said that she'd tried to find out from him when you were going to Hone. He wouldn't tell her but, of course, she could get it from the milkman or the paper boy. Or by just watching your movements. She probably remembers that you usually do go to the cottage for a few days about now."

Dee stared. Then she burst out laughing. "But what good would knowing that do her?"

"Don't laugh, Dee. That woman frightens me. She has some plan. I don't think she'd stop at anything to harm you."

Dee refused to take the matter seriously. "Carve me up, you mean? Throw acid into my face? Incarcerate me perhaps at the Limes? Come off it, Antonia!" She went on with unabated cheerfulness. "Now if I'd tried to get Sebastian Chant as far as the divorce court you would have something to worry about. Mirabella is quite a professional at repulsing girl friends—and with no holds barred. Her husband's favourites have to take their chance. Some are repelled at once. Others last longer. And I really do shudder at the thought of what would happen if Mirabella came up against someone as determined as herself."

Antonia had had to laugh at the picture conjured up of the twenty-two-year-old Dee in pursuit of the sexagenarian owner of Hone Court. Now she said, "I agree but I don't think it's her position Mirabella clings to. She really cares for Sebastian."

Dee nodded. "He's made a good few passes at me."

"Sebastian is always making a pass at someone." Antonia added to change the subject: "I wonder what the folk dancers are like this year?"

"Some of them will be fun. They always are. I couldn't stand even short blasts of rural life otherwise. Luckily Hone Court is madly popular with pop groups and all the odd bods and sods who make up the folk dance world. No, as long as the fine weather holds it will be all right. It's the first autumn rain that spoils things and makes them move out."

"One of these days it'll be the roof falling in. I know the Chants say the house will last their time but sometimes I wonder. I suppose it's having no children to inherit the place that makes them neglect it."

"There's a nephew somewhere," Dee remarked. "Now *he* showed every sign of becoming a super honey. When I was fifteen I thought he was fabulous."

"What happened to him?"

"When his father retired from the Army the family went out to New Zealand to live. The father died there and the widow decided to stay on. I don't know what happened to Michael. I didn't keep in touch."

Which was, Antonia reflected, typical of Dee. Her life seemed made up of friends and lovers who came unheralded and vanished, unmourned. She wondered, not for the first time, what had led to this oddly detached view of life. Or had Dee always been the same?

Dee glanced at her wristwatch. She stubbed out her cigarette. "Half-past twelve. I'd better be making a move if I'm going to do some shopping on the way down and still have time to take a look at the dancers by daylight to sort out the boys from the girls."

She was wearing a pale yellow suit in chamois leather with a baker-boy cap. Now she picked up her short fur coat and, after a moment's hesitation, the midday edition of the *Evening Standard* that had been lying on the table.

"I'd better hang on to this. The way things are going I may be reduced to watching television this evening. Then, at least, I'll have the programmes."

Antonia smiled. "Not much chance of that. Still, I do hope you won't be lured away by one of your dishy-looking pickups and not be at Hone when I get there."

"No pickups for me. My luck is right out. Perhaps Judith Harker has managed to ill wish me after all."

They asked for their bill and began to thread their way between the tables towards the cash desk, Dee walking with her easy stride, her clear brown eyes raking the sea of attentive faces. She was a natural blonde. A big girl who quite overshadowed her companion who was small and slightly built with sleek dark hair worn short, an oval face, a creamy complexion and dark blue, almost violet eyes.

There was a great deal of character in Antonia's face and, for the discerning, there would be little difficulty in imagining their respective roles. Dee casual, lighthearted, and irresponsible. Endlessly in trouble of her own making. Her friend levelheaded, prudent, and intelligent acting as ballast to her more volatile companion.

While Dee paid the bill Antonia looked casually back across the restaurant. Her heart missed a beat, for there, sitting alone at a table in an alcove that up to now had hidden her from the girls' sight, was Judith Harker.

She was a dark, haggard-looking woman of about forty. She was plainly but expensively dressed. Her complexion was weather-beaten and devoid of make-up. She had a tall lean figure and hard, clear-cut features. Her expression, Antonia thought, would have frightened anyone.

Oblivious of her surroundings she was staring at Dee, her

face disfigured by a look of the utmost hatred and malignity.

As the two girls left the restaurant Antonia saw that Mrs. Harker was rising from her seat. As they walked towards the decaying back street in which Dee had left her car Antonia glanced over her shoulder several times but saw no sign of pursuit. She wondered whether she should tell Dee of Mrs. Harker's presence in the restaurant. She decided against it. She felt certain that the woman was still somewhere nearby and that, provoked, Dee was quite capable of going in search of her, in which case they might all make the headlines again.

They turned a corner and there was the car. It was a very old, roomy two-seater known as the Bug. Its owner preferred it to the middle-price-range saloon she could have afforded. She argued rightly that if a ten-thousand-pound car was conspicuous then, at the other end of the scale, so was the Bug. Its battered chassis with a voluptuous blonde behind the driving wheel was guaranteed to catch every eye as it churned its way through the London streets. It was a joke of a car. The subject of endless pleasantries. An obliging car which would break down when required or speed merrily, if noisily, down byways and motorways alike.

Antonia reminded Dee that although there were plenty of tins in the store cupboard at the cottage, she would need to get in milk, bread, butter, bacon, and cheese. She added that she wanted her to buy a pint tin of Vesuvian as well.

"Vesuvian? Never heard of it," Dee declared, getting into her car. "Sounds a bit fiery. What is it?"

"It's for taking off old paint. Burning it off perhaps. Don't you remember we decided that the front door wanted repainting before the winter?"

"So we did. Don't count on me for any of the actual work. But I'll get the paint stripper tomorrow, if I have to go into Winstead to do it." Dee started the engine. She waved to Antonia. "See you on Saturday," she called and drove away.

Antonia stood staring after her. Wondering where Mrs. Harker was. Whether perhaps the Ford Anglia was even then preparing to fall in behind the Bug as it made its way towards the Kent coast.

As she turned away she realised that the day had grown grey and sad. That now the yellow head was the only bright speck in the dreary scene. She did not know exactly when the sun had gone, but its disappearance added to the vague melancholy and uneasiness she felt.

If only Dee had been less forthcoming in the witness box, she thought. If only Mrs. Harker had been less venomous and George Harker less well-known in the City. And, last of all, if only that wretched reporter from the *Daily Record* had been hump-backed, club-footed, or even deadly dull.

It had been a miserable business.

George Harker, usually a self-assured, even an impressive figure, had made a pathetic if slightly ridiculous appearance in the witness box, torn as he had been between differing loyalties. His respect for his wife and his infatuation for his mistress. Ex-mistress, as Dee had explained cheerfully. She had made no secret of the fact that, as far as she was concerned, the affair was over. Had been over for some time. Had never been worth all the fuss that was being made, the unhappy George not being all that exciting as a lover.

His wife, hard-faced and tight-lipped, had had her evidence corroborated by the detective whom she had hired to watch her husband. The judge had commented dryly and unfavourably on modern morality. The marriage between George and Judith Harker had been legally terminated. And Dee had returned, unrepentant, to the flat in Chelsea which she shared with Antonia.

The two girls had met at a dress show some three years before. Dee had been modelling the more daring of the frocks. Antonia had been gaining experience as a salesgirl and general dogsbody, before opening what had proved to be a most successful boutique of her own. They had liked each other at first sight. Later they had decided to set up house together. Although poles apart in character they had got on surprisingly well.

During the three years Antonia had grown very fond of her flatmate. She worried about her because, as she pointed out, there was no one else to do so, Dee being an orphan with not a relation in the world.

At the back of Antonia's mind there had grown up over the years an unexpressed and indeed largely unacknowledged fear. It was that Dee, so casual, so undiscriminating, might fall into the hands of some faceless monster. That her lovely body might one day be found raped and mutilated, lying on a bleak and unfrequented common. Fished perhaps from a lonely stretch of still, dark water.

Now, as she waited for her bus, Antonia had a new, more pressing fear. The faceless monster had been replaced by the more familiar and avenging figure of Judith Harker.

And yet what could Mrs. Harker do? Make a public scene? Dee would laugh her head off. Offer physical violence? Dee was young, healthy, and strong. More than a match for the older woman.

So why worry?

But worry Antonia did—all Thursday evening. And at odd intervals during Friday when business had slackened. Nor was her anxiety lessened by the fact that she had telephoned the Thatched Cottage several times without getting a reply. Had stood hearing the bell ringing and ringing as if in an empty house.

On Saturday Antonia awoke late and in a cheerful frame of mind. The morning had she told herself brought with it a needed sense of proportion. The boutique was closed for a fortnight. By four o'clock that afternoon she would have reached the Thatched Cottage. There she would find Dee. Or if not Dee then a communication from her.

She went into the kitchen and made herself a cup of tea, drinking it while she stood staring idly out of the window. Then she fetched the morning paper from the hall and went back to bed.

She was startled to see that there was news of Hone on the front page. It was headed, TRAGEDY AT SEA! It read:

> Disaster overtook three friends holidaying in the Winstead area, who set out on a two-hour fishing trip early

yesterday evening. The body of one of the young men, Claud Greenwood, was recovered from inside the hull of the upturned boat. A second body, that of Keith Vesey, had by some freak been carried on to the notorious Race Rocks and was found wedged there. The third member of the party, David Price, is still missing.

It is thought that in the sea mist that came down suddenly yesterday evening the boat must have gone on to the rocks. It was not seen until first light next morning when a coastguard spotted it upside down at the foot of the cliffs near Hone. Its outboard motor was missing and there was a long crack in the hull.

The Race Rocks, some fifty yards from the shore and practically invisible at high tide, are well known to be dangerous. Not only because of their razor-edged formation but because of the very strong currents that flow around them.

The names of the three young men who had lost their lives were all strange to Antonia. Her first thought, of which she was immediately ashamed, was that this disaster so much more dramatic and calamitous, would divert interest from Dee's new-found notoriety. She recalled how often she had stood among the sea pinks at the cliff edge watching the water as it boiled and bubbled about the grim sawlike rocks.

Gruesome, she thought, and, shivering a little, slid farther under the bedclothes. Presently she went to sleep again.

The newspaper account was read by Detective Inspector Engleman. He sat in his room at the Winstead Police Station, his feet on his desk.

His first thought was that the story, although brief, contained all the known facts. This was followed by the reflection that the publicity would do Hone no good and might even drive away some of its visitors. Lucky it was the end of the season—

At this point Engleman had a third and more cheerful thought. He took his feet off the desk. He picked up the telephone and asked to be put through to New Scotland Yard. He wanted to speak to Detective Chief Inspector Finch.

The two men had been friends for some ten years, having met accidentally during a near riot at a football match. Later, treating cuts and bruises, they had been amused to find that they followed the same calling. Later still, they had discovered a mutual passion for golf. Since then they had often played together, latterly on the fine new golf course opened at Winstead to add to the attractions of that popular seaside resort.

Their friendship had not been affected by Finch's advance in seniority nor by the fact that he was one of those police officers whom the public take to its heart. Engleman was not a jealous man but he did sometimes have a horrid dream in which his friend, while looking in the rough for a ball, came upon a sanguinary corpse.

When the two men had exchanged greetings, Engleman said, "Septimus, you remember you tried to get down here for a few days golf?"

"Vividly, dear boy. All the Winstead hotels were booked up." The answering voice was very clear but soft and drawling.

"I think you might have a chance now to get into the Bull's Head at Hone. You've probably read about the drowning of those three young men? Yes, well Hone is noted for its safe bathing and it struck me that anyone a bit squeamish might cut short his holiday and go home. After all, one poor chap is still washing about in the sea."

"It's a ghoulish thought but worth following up. I suppose it wouldn't apply to Winstead as well?"

"You take my advice and stick to Hone." Engleman sounded amused. "It's not generally known but a certain fair celebrity arrived here on Thursday last."

Finch's mind ran over the fair celebrities he knew in the course of business. "Ben, are you suggesting I combine business with pleasure?" he asked suspiciously.

Engleman laughed. "I can look after my own celebrities of that character, thank you very much. No, I was talking about the delectable Miss Delia Sumner."

Finch gave a low wolf-whistle and then demanded how Engleman knew.

"The local rag—it's keeping tabs on her. She was born and brought up in Hone and still has the cottage her parents left her." Engleman added reflectively: "I should think she'd be thankful to have somewhere to hide."

"Not that young woman. I suspect that to her the whole thing was one great big laugh. No, it's Mrs. Harker who must feel like going into hiding. The reporting of divorce cases is pretty firmly controlled but the articles that appeared in the *Daily Record* make one wonder whether the laws of libel don't want altering. It was indecent what was done to her."

"Now that *was* one great big laugh, although Mrs. Harker is hardly the type to appreciate it."

"Then you know her?"

"I've seen her around—at the local gymkhanas and county horse shows. She comes of an old Irish family. One of those hard-faced, stingy-sporting types. She's a good shot too."

"Sounds a formidable woman. Any chance she might go gunning for Miss Sumner?"

"No, we shan't see her in these parts again," Engleman answered cheerfully. "Not that she isn't capable of violence. About twelve months ago she was had up for using her riding whip on a man she caught ill-treating a horse."

Finch's gently murmuring voice came down the line: "Ben, you fill me with alarm on the girl's behalf."

Engleman laughed. "Don't you go offering her yourself as police protection. Superintendent Bollard wouldn't like it."

After lunch Antonia packed a suitcase. Then recalling past experiences she added the remains of a wholemeal loaf, a wedge of Dutch cheese, and half a pound of butter to the contents of the roomy shoulder bag she was taking with her.

Where Dee was concerned it was as well to be prepared. Such things as avocado pears, *marrons glacés*—of which Dee was inordinately fond—and even caviar, gift of one of her rich admirers, might be awaiting Antonia at the Thatched Cottage. The small change of housekeeping might well be absent.

It was a good train service to Winstead. Antonia reached it at half-past three. There she caught the local bus to Hone. She was thankful to see that, as often happened at this time of year, the half-dozen passengers were strangers to her, being summer visitors.

She settled down contentedly staring out of the dusty window at the lovely Kentish countryside. London seemed very far away. The boutique and its problems belonged to another life. Even Mrs. Harker no longer seemed to threaten.

The bus put her down at the beginning of the lane that led to the Thatched Cottage. Now there were fields and cows on one side and the woods of Hone Court on the other. The air felt clear and fresh. Antonia drew in a deep breath. She felt hungry. As she walked along with her suitcase she visualised the roomy picturesque cottage, the kettle boiling, a big tea laid in the sitting room and Dee smiling at the front door.

She turned a corner and the cottage appeared in sight. She came to a halt, staring. And, silent and secretive looking, with every window closed and the door shut fast, it seemed to stare back at her. Her heart sank. Dee was not there. By the look of it had never been there. As Antonia pushed open the garden gate and walked up the narrow path, she was conscious of a growing sense of anxiety and disaster.

The front door opened directly into the one long room, half-dining, half-sitting room. For a moment Antonia's heart lifted. She thought that Dee, incurably untidy, had arrived after all; for on an old oak chest lay a miscellaneous collection of articles belonging to her. A newspaper, a leather belt, a pair of shoes, a box of chocolates, and a silver bracelet.

"Dee!" Antonia called. The room gave back a faint empty echo and no more.

Antonia picked up the newspaper. She saw now that it was not the one Dee had had with her when she had left London two days ago. This one was yellowing at the edges and was dated 2nd July, the date when she had been last in the cottage.

Under the newspaper were two sheets of paper torn from a notebook and pinned together. On the top sheet was written:

Miss Dee, these things were left lying about. The chocolates you'd better throw away. You left the lid off and the flies will have been on them, the nasty dirty things.

The second sheet was a bill for work done in the cottage.

Thursday, 27th July, three hours work, 90 new pence.
Tuesday, 29th August, 4 hours work £1-20.
                                        Signed *Doris Epps.*

Mrs. Epps looked after the cottage during its owner's absence. Before her marriage to the local baker's roundsman she had been Dee's nurse. She still refused to put away anything left about in the sitting room by her one-time nurseling. Instead, she collected them all in one place and left them as a silent rebuke. She also, Antonia reflected, had a thing about flies.

There were two staircases in the cottage since it had once been a pair of semi-detached dwelling places. One led to Dee's large bedroom, which had been her parents'. The other led to Antonia's smaller room and the spare bedroom.

Antonia ran up the stairs to her friend's room. As soon as she opened the door she realised the truth. Dee had never arrived at the cottage.

The room was too tidy. The drawers were neatly closed. The wardrobe doors were shut. No odd garments were strewn over the floor nor draped on the chairs. The bedspread was uncreased—and Dee always sat on the edge of the bed in preference to any more conventional seat.

That settles it, Antonia thought. Dee hasn't been here. Between London and Hone something happened to prevent her. And again she wondered uneasily whether that something could have been Mrs. Harker. And yet this was not the first time that Dee had failed to arrive as expected. Only—always before she had telephoned, written, or appeared in person, cheerful, unabashed, full of the account of some attractive male whom she had met on the way and with whom she had spent anything from a single night to a week.

Antonia considered ringing up the local police in the person of Police Constable Hobday. She was held back by visualising the amusement and barely concealed incredulity with which he would greet her enquiry.

Yet ought she, Antonia, to allow this probable reaction to sway her? Hobday would, if pressed, make the necessary enquiries. Discover whether any accident to the Bug or its owner had been reported.

She went to the telephone. P. C. Hobday sounded as incredulous as she had expected but she knew him well and could tell him of Mrs. Harker's strange behaviour and of her own fears. He did not sound impressed but he promised to make every enquiry.

"I'll ring you back in about half an hour, miss," he said. "And if I were you I wouldn't worry. Miss Dee will turn up when she's a mind to. You'll see."

This brisk normality had a cheering effect on Antonia. Amused Hobday might be but if he said that nothing dreadful had happened to Dee on the road then she would accept it as being true. Meanwhile, she assured herself, there was plenty to do to pass the time.

She saw Dee's possessions still lying on the chest. She opened the box of chocolates. They certainly didn't look very appetising, although this was due, she suspected, to the heat of the closed room rather than to flies. She carried the box and the out-of-date newspaper through the house and threw them into the empty dustbin outside the back door.

The other things she collected and took with her to her own room. It was less trouble. Dee could have them when she arrived.

Antonia made up her bed. She dusted the room. She unpacked. Then carrying the bread, butter, and cheese down to the kitchen, she opened a tin of condensed milk and made herself some coffee.

There was a breakfast recess in the kitchen. Dee, when alone, had her meals there on the grounds that it was less trouble. Antonia, under the same circumstances, took hers into the sitting room. She found it more comfortable. She did not sit at the dining table. She preferred the couch, slender brown legs drawn up under her, tray on the low coffee table in front of her.

She put the tray down. She crossed the floor to the record player. There was a record already on the turntable. She saw to her surprise that it was not one of hers, although she knew the music well. It was the Fantasy Overture to Tchaikovsky's *Romeo and Juliet*, played by the Vienna Philharmonic Orchestra.

Antonia smiled to herself. It had not been Dee's choice, that was certain. It must have been played by someone whom she had had in the cottage when she had been down that weekend in July. And, poor creature, he would not have got far with his record.

She switched it on. Adjusted the volume and went back to curl up on the settee. When the music had ended it seemed to leave a faint residue of sadness behind it.

Antonia found herself speculating about the person who had brought the record into the cottage. Where had Dee been when he had attempted to play it, she wondered? Anywhere within hearing and she would have been shouting for something more cheerful to be put on. Something with a bit of go in it—preferably the latest song to have headed the charts.

In Antonia's uneasy mind the music sounded again. Dee's protesting voice called in the distance and a shadow stirred across the room beside the record player.

For a moment the cottage seemed full of ghosts.

TWO

The telephone rang suddenly and stridently in the sitting room. Hobday or Dee? Antonia sprang up and seized the receiver. "Yes?" she cried anxiously. "Yes?"

It was P. C. Hobday. The police at Winstead had, he assured her, made exhaustive enquiries. No accident to a car resembling the Bug had been reported. No one answering to Dee's description had been taken to any hospital. "In fact, miss, a constable on point duty in Charing remembers seeing both car and driver going through the town early Thursday afternoon. So she was all right then. It must have been after this that Miss Sumner—deviated." This last word seemed to amuse him and he said it with relish.

Antonia thanked him with dignity and rang off. So that was all right, she told herself. Dee was somewhere safe. She would telephone now that Antonia was at the cottage. Or appear in person.

Antonia carried her tray into the kitchen. Got her bicycle out of the otherwise empty garage and set off at a good pace in the direction of Hone to do the shopping.

A little way along the main road was a gleaming white-painted wooden gate. It was the entrance to the Limes, a solid

Georgian house with a handsome portico and long sash windows. A three- or four-servant house. In happier times the Harkers had brought their London staff down with them.

It came as a shock to Antonia to see the tall spare figure of the woman who had been so much in her thoughts at a closed upstair window. Mrs. Harker was standing, it seemed to the girl, unnaturally still, her gaze fixed on the distant view. The whole pose of the motionless figure bore an uncomfortable suggestion of patient vigilance that Antonia found unnerving.

At Hone all the talk was still of the tragedy that had taken place at sea. Antonia learnt that two of the young men had been staying at the Grand Hotel in Winstead for the last three weeks. The third, Keith Vesey, had with a friend, Roger Frampton, rented a furnished cottage from the Chants since the end of June. It stood about a mile farther along the coast. These two had been known as the rich Mr. Frampton and poor Mr. Vesey. This had alluded to the wealth of the one and the poor health of the other.

She was told a dozen theories as to how the boat came to go upon the rocks, as the villagers picked over the few details with ghoulish repetition. To them the sea had always been treacherous. It was easy to identify themselves with the sadness and shock of unexpected death. They could enter into the unknown Mrs. Vesey's feelings. She was not the only widowed mother to lose her son.

Antonia was told again of the grief of the survivor. How Roger Frampton had refused to open the front door or answer the telephone. How later he had walked endlessly backwards and forwards along the seashore, as if watching for the return of the last of his friends.

There was even a story, told originally by Tom Epps to his mother. It was that at night he had seen Roger Frampton running in a distraught way over the downs on the far side of Treadle Bay. That he had thrown out his arms and legs. Cried out in a loud, strange voice. And then had run on harder than before.

In the ordinary way not much credence would have been

(18)

given to this tale, since Tom Epps was simple. Now it appeared a natural expression of the young man's grief.

Antonia told herself that this sole survivor of the tragic quartette needed only the service of a strolling minstrel to become a legend in the Kentish countryside. Certainly he seemed fitted for the role, if half she heard of him were true. He was rich, tall, handsome, charming. He was—or had been —gay and amusing.

Her shopping finished, Antonia rode slowly along the road on her way back to the cottage. At the foot of the hill she dismounted and began to push the bicycle.

She heard footsteps behind her. A pleasant, rather deep male voice remarked: "If you don't mind my saying so, you're going to lose the load on your carrier."

Antonia turned. It was true. Her purchases, never very secure, had worked loose. She looked at the speaker. She saw a young man, tall, lithe, and muscular. He had dark hair, steady grey eyes, a narrow jaw, and a long humorous mouth.

Dee's ideal man, Antonia thought, and she was not there to appreciate the fact. The idea amused Antonia. Her eyes sparkled. Her lips curved delightedly. The smile she bestowed on the young man appeared far more welcoming than it would otherwise have been.

"I see what you mean," she admitted. "I suppose I should have made two journeys. Or waited until my friend arrived with her car."

"Your parcels should be all right now." The young man had deftly repacked the various articles. He was looking at Antonia with open admiration. "Have you far to go?"

"As far as the Thatched Cottage down the lane at the top of the hill." Not a muscle of the young man's face changed. He looked serious now, even solemn, too solemn perhaps. Antonia watched him suspiciously. She supposed there were people who had not read those wretched articles. But, if so, she had not met them.

"Are you staying long?" His pleasant voice broke in on her thoughts.

"A fortnight." Antonia added repressively: "I've come down for a rest."

"A rest? Then let me push the bike. I'm going your way back to Hone Court."

"Are you one of the dancers?"

"I used to come here when I was a boy and dance my legs off. Can't do it now. I picked up some sort of bug in New Guinea. That cramps my style a bit."

"I *am* sorry," said Antonia. Dee had no patience with ill health.

He smiled down at her. "Not to worry. The Hospital for Tropical Diseases has done a wonderful job on me. They say they'll soon be able to give me a clean bill of health."

"Good! So you're at the Court convalescing?"

"Yes, since my home is in New Zealand and the Chants are my relations it seemed the best thing to do. I'm Michael Chant, their nephew."

The nephew from New Zealand! The man whom Dee had once thought of as fabulous and, no doubt, would do so again.

"How extraordinary that we should meet," she said slowly. "Dee mentioned you for the first time only last Thursday."

Michael's smile broadened. "Still the same old Dee. No past. No future. Only the present." They were opposite the Limes. He glanced at it briefly. "Does she know that Mrs. Harker is down here?"

"She expected it." Antonia was thankful to see that no one stood now at the window.

"It's going to be a bit awkward, isn't it?" His gaze was indolent but sharp. "Given Mrs. Harker's present frame of mind."

"It's going to be more than awkward." Antonia explained how Dee had been followed in London. How Mrs. Harker had tried to get information about her movements from the porter. "And when I passed the house on my way to the village," she ended, "there she was at an upstair window staring out."

"Watching the end of the lane for Dee's appearance, I suppose."

Antonia looked at him with horror. "I never thought of that," she said.

Inside the Thatched Cottage, Michael looked about him with interest.

"It is a jolly cottage. Except for new covers and curtains it doesn't seem to have changed at all," he remarked. "I always thought it one of the nicest conversions. But then Mr. Sumner was an architect. And a pretty good one too."

Antonia nodded. Dee's parents had both died in an influenza epidemic seven years before. They were a somewhat shadowy couple, for Dee seldom mentioned them. Antonia had often wondered why. Had she not cared for them perhaps? Or cared too much?

"Dee is very like her father," Michael went on. "A blond giant of a man, very handsome, good natured, and tolerant. He adored his wife. I can imagine that when he knew that she had died he didn't bother to go on living."

He had been roaming about the room as he spoke, looking at this and that. Now picking up a remembered ornament. Now bending his head to read the title of a book in the low shelves. His long, lean figure had, Antonia thought, a rather impressive distinction. It was difficult to imagine him so closely related to the dumpy, blue-eyed Chants of Hone Court.

"Dee hardly ever mentioned her parents," she remarked.

"I suppose not. She was always the odd one out. They were fond of her but she was never necessary to their happiness."

"I think that's very sad," said Antonia slowly. She was wondering if it explained Dee's gift of complete disregard of other people's opinions and her capacity for living entirely in the present.

Michael looked at her, amused. "Dee had her own pleasures. Even at fifteen she was quite a girl."

"I still think it sad." Antonia invited him to have a drink but he refused.

"I ought to be getting back to the Court. Why don't you come with me? My uncle and aunt would be delighted. They have been half-expecting you for some time now."

Antonia agreed. The Chants, she knew, kept open house. "I'll just wash my hands and change. You amuse yourself. I shan't be long."

She left him still wandering nostalgically about the room. When she came downstairs he was sitting in one of the deep armchairs reading a book.

Antonia was wearing slim black trousers and a jerkin vaguely heraldic in design and richness of colour.

Michael saw her. He sprang to his feet. "I say! You look like a mediaeval page," he cried admiringly, throwing down the book.

Antonia laughed. "I know, Agincourt and all that."

They left the cottage, walking up the lane. There was a footpath to Hone Court. It led across a field and then through the woods. They strolled along, talking easily. She asked him what he had been doing in New Guinea and learnt that he was a social anthropologist. Observing, as he said, how Stone Age man coped with the coming of technological man and the consequent clash of cultures.

Still talking, they emerged from the woods into a walled space, once part of the kitchen garden but now a car park. Here there was a variety of cars. Most of them were shabby. Some of them were decrepit. The newer ones were shrouded in tarpaulins to save them from the attentions of the fowls who scratched and pecked around them by day and roosted on them by night.

Hone Court itself had been erected in the middle of the eighteenth century. The date of its completion, 1753, was carved on the chimney piece of what had once been known as the Green Drawing Room. It was an ornate building with large semicircular windows in front. It had a handsome lead-covered octagonal dome, an equally handsome portico, a wide terrace of red and white tiles and a long row of life-size statues.

Originally an impressive sight, the paint on the house was now flaking from doors and window frames. Pigeons, from wherever they could obtain a perch on the ornate façade, had picked the mortar from between the rosy bricks. The red and white tiles were badly chipped and the statues had lost an ear, a nose, a hand, or, in one case, the entire head which it now cradled in the crook of its arm. However, in the warm glow of the setting sun the general impression was imposing enough.

There was a wide sweep of grass beyond the tiled terrace. Here some twenty young people were dancing. There was a little knot of spectators. Antonia and her companion joined them.

"There you are, Michael," said a woman's voice just behind them. "I was going to ask you—" The voice broke off as Antonia turned to see who was speaking. She found herself staring up into Mrs. Harker's angry, dark eyes.

"Never mind, Michael. I can ask you when you're less busy." Judith Harker walked swiftly away towards the house.

Sebastian Chant, who was standing watching the dancers, saw Antonia and her escort. He waved cheerfully and came towards them. He looked younger than his age which was sixty. He was short and podgy. He had an all-over pink complexion and round, rather innocent-looking blue eyes.

"Hullo, Antonia, my dear." He bent and kissed her on the cheek. "Welcome back. So you've met my nephew, have you."

Antonia smiled at him affectionately. She had a soft spot for both the Chants. "Michael came to my rescue on Stoddart Hill when my parcels looked like cascading to the ground."

Sebastian's grin broadened. "Trust him. Michael's always had an eye for a pretty girl. You should have seen him with Dee in the old days." He produced a large white handkerchief and mopped his forehead. "Been dancing most of the afternoon," he explained. Adding: "Where is Dee?"

"She hasn't arrived yet," which, Antonia reflected, was strictly true.

"The naughty puss! She put the cat among the pigeons all right. Still, come into the house. Mirabella will be delighted to see you." He lowered his naturally robust voice. "Judith Harker will probably be staying to supper. But, since you're bound to meet her, it may as well be here among friends, eh?"

"I've seen her already. And, as the old saying goes, if looks could kill, I'd have died right here on your front lawn."

"I don't imagine that Judith will make a scene in public," said Michael.

"Don't be too sure," Sebastian advised. "Judith's like a scalded cat."

The dance came to an end. A short, plump girl detached herself from the group. She came smiling across the lawn. Her thick reddish brown hair was parted in the centre and brought low over her ears to rest on her neck in a heavy coil, giving her a Burne-Jones look. She was wearing a long limp green frock and, Antonia saw, very little else. It was cut low at the back so that it showed a lot of plump flesh, sunburnt and blotched faintly with pale freckles.

"Ah, there's my girl," cried Sebastian, putting his arm around her shoulders. "Antonia, meet Beatrice Lynham. You two should get on well together."

"Than which there is no more certain way of ensuring the contrary," Michael declared, smiling at Antonia. Beatrice said nothing. Her hazel eyes were appraising and faintly hostile.

The four of them walked round the house and in by a side door. Sebastian and his wife, Mirabella, occupied only one wing, the rest being given up to the dancers. They did most of their entertaining in a kitchen made by throwing two rooms into one. It was all very functional but comfortable and convenient.

Mirabella Chant was busy at the Aga cooker. She had an acute face, a quizzical expression and bright, protruding eyes like those of a clever pug dog. To look at she was short and largely spherical. Her head was round. The mouse-coloured bun which topped it was round. Her bosom was rounded and so was her firm little behind.

She was wearing a high-waisted, peasant style frock in very bright colours. White stockings covered her plump calves and her small feet were thrust into heelless black slippers.

She was a woman who responded to life dramatically. She spoke with emphasis. She made wide expansive gestures like an old-fashioned actress.

She beamed when she saw Antonia. "My de-ah child! At last!" To hear her no one would have guessed that they had had lunch together in London not six weeks ago. She folded the girl in her arms.

There was always, Antonia reflected, returning her embrace, a nice fresh smell like a baby about Mirabella.

Sebastian and his nephew went over to the side table where

the drinks were, after enquiring what everyone would have. Beatrice sank down artistically on the rug close to Sebastian's chair.

Judith Harker came into the room. She was wearing a sage green trouser suit and an orange blouse. The colours made her look more sallow than ever. Her expression was forbidding, her gaze bleak. Antonia noticed, without surprise, that Mirabella, who kissed nearly everyone, made no attempt to kiss her.

"There you are, Judith," she cried. "Just in time for supper. But, before I forget, I shall be alone here tomorrow evening, since our young people are dancing in Winstead. So do come over." Adding optimistically: "Come early, about five. Then we can have a nice long cosy evening together."

"Thank you. I'd like that." Judith's tone of voice sounded flat, automatic. Far less enthusiastic than the words would have suggested.

"Splendid!" Mirabella looked about her. She added, in a spritely voice, "You know everyone here I think. Beatrice Lynham, quite one of our most *aspiring* dancers. Miss Hughes, you must have met—although you two are seldom in Hone at the same time."

"Indeed no," said Judith icily. "It was Miss Sumner who seemed always to arrive when my husband and I were at the Limes."

"Dee comes down here far more often than I do," Antonia answered. "But then she looks on it as home."

"Miss Sumner was here last Thursday," said Judith in a voice that allowed of no argument.

"Dee *intended* to be here last Thursday," Antonia corrected. She was determined not to be intimidated. "She is always a bit erratic. But she should be down any day now."

Judith Harker smiled unpleasantly. "Are you certain she didn't arrive last Thursday and leave again—for fear of meeting me?"

"But Dee isn't afraid of you."

Judith fixed the younger woman with a curiously blank and glittering stare. "Then I think she should be."

Something about the dark expressionless gaze sent a shiver

through Antonia. "If you cared so much for your marriage you shouldn't have broken it up. Dee never wanted that," she said stiffly.

While this exchange had been going on Mirabella had been busy taking plates and dishes from one of the large ovens of the Aga cooker and putting them on top of the stove. Now, wearing a pair of gay cooking gloves, she lifted an enormous casserole and carried it towards the dining table.

"Michael, will you bring the vegetables and salad?"

As she approached the recumbent Beatrice she appeared to stumble. For one terrifying moment the steaming casserole seemed on the point of falling. The next it had been righted.

"What a clumsy old woman I am," Mirabella cried, rolling her bulging eyes. "I nearly dropped the whole thing. Why, Beatrice, you look quite pale."

The girl gave her a look of furious dislike. "You did it on purpose to frighten me."

"Hoity, toity, miss! Why should I want to do that?" Mirabella, a smug look on her face, circled the girl. She held the casserole high over her head. It was a pose that vaguely suggested a small eccentric goddess of plenty complete with cornucopia.

They all seated themselves at the table.

Sebastian, serving the vegetables, remarked with the gusto he brought to all his activities, "There was some truth in what Antonia said, Judith, little as you may like to admit it. Middle-aged men, however foolishly they may behave, don't wish to break up their homes."

Judith looked at him. "Are you suggesting that I should have stood meekly by waiting for Miss Sumner to finish her affair with my husband?"

Said Sebastian bluntly, "If you wanted to save your marriage—yes."

"Then I would be waiting still," declared Judith bitterly.

"But Dee broke with your husband long ago," Antonia declared. She was pale. This public wrangle was horrible.

Judith laughed mirthlessly. "But has my husband broken with her? I doubt it."

"One has to be patient," Mirabella joined in, resting her plump elbows on the table and cushioning her chin in her hands. "George has the greatest respect for you, Judith. That is half the battle."

"I am not as complaisant as you are," Judith answered sullenly. She was not eating, although she made a pretence of doing so.

"You're not as sensible. Nor," said Sebastian, bowing handsomely to his wife, "as kind."

Judith's thin lips thinned still further. "I cannot see a wife's duty as Mirabella does."

"What a pity," said Mirabella. "I think one wants to decide, right at the beginning of married life, what one wants most out of it. If it is to keep your husband then you must do something about it." She added coaxingly, "Couldn't you forgive George?"

"The poor fellow looks quite broken up," Sebastian added.

"I might have known you'd be on his side," Judith said bitterly. She stood up, pushing back her chair with an irritable gesture.

"You're not going? Just when we were having such an interesting discussion."

"I can see no reason for staying." Judith glared around the table. "And don't waste your time being sorry for *me*. I have ways of getting my own back." She spoke these last two sentences with such vicious malignity that every one was momentarily shocked into silence.

Michael, with a rueful glance at his aunt, threw down his napkin and hurried from the room in pursuit of their departing guest.

Mirabella stared after her. "So much for the theory that to bring things out into the open has a therapeutic effect."

"The woman's dangerous," Sebastian declared. He looked shaken and alarmed.

Beatrice burst out laughing. "What a temper." She looked across the table at Antonia. "I can't help feeling that I'd be a little nervous if I were your friend."

Sebastian nodded. "Beatrice is right. And, since the female

of the species is deadlier than the male, it might be as well if Dee didn't come here just at present."

"I couldn't agree more," Antonia assured him. "The trouble is that Dee isn't at the flat. I've no way of getting in touch with her."

"When she does come," said Mirabella comfortably, "we must persuade her to go away again—perhaps with Michael."

The young man returned in time to hear his aunt's suggestion. "I must decline," he said promptly, "on the grounds of a prior attachment."

"How inconsiderate of you," Mirabella declared. "And you used to be such friends. However, it will sort itself out. You'll see. And after all Dee has been a teeny, weeny bit naughty."

Her husband gave a snort of amusement. "And so deserved a teeny, weeny punishment, eh?"

The meal progressed. The subject of the Harkers and Dee was dropped. The conversation became more cheerful.

The bell on the outer door rang shrilly. This was followed by the sound of approaching footsteps. The door opened. Two people stood there, looking in.

The first was a young woman very tall and slim, wearing a small cloche hat and a long dark cloak. She was fair. Not so much blond as colourless. Her grey eyes were dark circled, the lids veined with blue and almost transparent. She looked tense, tragic, and dropping with fatigue. Behind her, gazing soberly over her shoulder, was one of the handsomest, most romantic-looking young men Antonia had ever seen. "The door wasn't locked," he said in a low, pleasant voice. "We just walked in."

Michael sprang to his feet. "Roger, my dear chap!"

Mirabella surged forward. "And you must be Clare," she cried. She kissed the girl soundly. Then drew back to look at her, holding her strong, rather angular hands in her own plump paws. "You would be very welcome in any case. You are doubly welcome because you look at us with your brother's grey eyes. He had become very dear to us."

"He had indeed." Sebastian had dispossessed his wife of one of Clare Vesey's hands. He shook it solemnly. "A splendid fellow. The world will be the poorer for his going."

(28)

"You are very kind," said the pale Miss Vesey.

"I was on my way here," Roger explained, "when I ran into Clare. She had come down in answer to my letter and had just been turned from the last of Hone's three pubs. They are all full up and she didn't seem in a fit state to go looking for a room anywhere else."

"Roger insisted on bringing me but I do realise it is the most dreadful imposition." Miss Vesey spoke very fast in a soft exhausted yet somehow frantic-sounding voice. She looked at no one and clutched her dark cloak about her as if it were her last defence against a hostile world.

"Roger was quite right," said Mirabella warmly. "Of course you must stay here. There is lots of room and you are most welcome."

"We should have tried the cottages," said Clare, as if Mirabella had not spoken. "I told Roger so. He said it was too late but I don't give in so easily. No, I do not give in so easily."

"Hush, my dear. If only for Keith's sake you must stay with us. He would have wished it." Mirabella was detaching Clare's fingers one by one from her cloak as she spoke. "The only thing left to be decided is whether you would prefer to go to bed now and have your supper brought up to you? Or whether you will stay down here and give us the pleasure of your company?"

"I'll stay down here, please. I am not in any hurry to go to bed." Clare took off her small hat. She ran her fingers through her silk-like hair. "I should like to stay up all night."

"Just what I should have suggested," Mirabella agreed. She spoke as if it were the most pleasant prospect in the world. "But first you must have something to eat."

Introductions followed. Two more places were laid at table. Clare sat by her hostess, although Antonia could not decide whether this had been Clare's decision or Mirabella's. Roger sat next to Beatrice and across the table from Antonia.

Sebastian, declaring that he knew just what was wanted to restore Clare after her journey, hurried from the room. He was going to fetch a bottle of champagne. He was glad to escape for a time. He knew a distraught woman when he saw one.

As soon as supper was over Mirabella took Clare to her bedroom to, as she put it, freshen up. Sebastian insisted on following with his guest's suitcase. He had dropped his usual approach of jovial dalliance. He was subdued and, when he looked at Clare, his eyes grieved for her.

When he returned Roger said apologetically, "I hope you don't mind my coming here, sir? When the coastguards turned up again like ruddy vultures I just couldn't take any more."

Michael glanced at him sympathetically. "High tide, you mean? I can imagine it's been a bit grim."

"Trouble is," said Sebastian, "that bodies always do come ashore sooner or later at Treadle Bay. Matter of the currents. It'll be a relief when this last poor chap does turn up and the inquest can be held."

"You can say that again," said Roger fervently. "Once that is over and poor old Keith has been buried I'll be off as fast and as far as I can go."

Sebastian looked at him from under his somewhat untidy eyebrows. "And Clare?"

Roger sighed. "Clare's wonderful—but I'm beginning to realise that she can do without me. Fact is," he confided moodily, "I'm beginning to think that she can do without anyone. Her work seems enough for her."

"She has a most attractive and unusual face," Antonia remarked. "What does she do?"

"She's a portrait painter," Roger answered in a fond voice. "A pretty good one. Her work is already beginning to attract attention."

"She has a sort of luminous look," Antonia went on. "Almost as if there were a light burning somewhere inside her."

Roger's face shadowed. "I know. Poor old Keith had it too."

"I remember that charcoal portrait of him his sister did. The one you have over the mantelpiece at Treadle Bay Cottage," said Michael. "It really is a first-class bit of work."

Roger nodded. He lowered his voice. "She seems to have some crazy idea of going to the mortuary and seeing Keith."

Sebastian gave a shocked exclamation. "She mustn't do that. She'd never forget it. The sight might haunt her for life."

"You try telling her," Roger answered feelingly. He passed

a well-shaped hand over his face in a frustrated way. "The whole business makes me feel a heel," he muttered.

"Why on earth should it?" Michael demanded. "None of it was your fault."

Roger looked somewhat shamefaced. "When I was walking here with Clare I couldn't help feeling that she had changed towards me. Almost as if she felt I'd no business to be alive when Keith was dead."

"Rot, old man," said Michael vigorously. "From all accounts Clare is far too nice a person to entertain any such idea."

"For Heaven's sake," Beatrice cried shrilly, "don't let's begin on Clare again. I had enough of it from Keith. Clare is so clever. Clare is such a good manager. Clare is so beautiful. Clare is so altogether wonderful." Her voice rose still further. "Personally Clare makes me sick."

"What a fat little stinker you are, Beatrice," Michael declared in an interested voice. "How do you manage to be so consistent?"

"Don't you call me fat," Beatrice cried. She went on venomously: "It was bad enough having everyone talking about those three idiotic young men. Now we're to have one of their bereaved relations actually staying here. We'll be expected to mind our words. Tread softly and go about with long faces."

"Not at all," said Michael smoothly. "I can't see that Clare is likely to interfere with your enjoyment or that of the other dancers."

Beatrice glared at him. "Meaning that I should keep to my own part of the house?"

Sebastian chuckled. "Got you there, Beatrice. And it's true. If you see anything of Clare Vesey it will be of your own choosing."

"But we were so happy as we were," Beatrice wailed. "Now it's all spoilt."

"It was spoilt for most of us last Thursday when the sea mist closed in," said Roger glowering at her.

"It's the one thing I don't like about Hone," Antonia remarked, glancing sympathetically at Roger. "I am always glad to get away from it and into the cottage."

Beatrice looked at her contemptuously. "How grotesque," she sneered. "Now I make a point of going out whenever it's really misty. There's a sort of unexpectedness about it. You never know what you are going to see."

"If anyone does see anything they aren't supposed to I imagine you would be the one to do it," said Michael reflectively.

"How right you are," said Beatrice with a shrill laugh.

THREE

The rest of the evening passed slowly, sometimes painfully. Clare came down again. She had changed into something soft and grey. Homemade Antonia's expert eye told her but it suited the older woman's slim elegance.

She seemed altogether quieter, almost tranquil. Perhaps, Antonia reflected, she was too worn out with shock and grief to be anything else. She spoke calmly and affectionately of her brother and of what they had been to each other. She showed a little of her former agitation when she spoke of her feelings of disbelief and horror when she had received Roger's letter. She did not mention the actual tragedy.

It was Roger who kept bringing it up, dwelling on the circumstances in every painful detail. Watching Clare covertly yet intently as he did so.

"They were going to try their luck fishing. Keith said he'd bring back our breakfast . . .

"It was a new boat. A blue and white Fiberglas hull. The sea was calm . . .

"It was nearly half-past eleven when I rang up the Grand intending to ask Keith whether he was sleeping at the hotel.

It was only when none of the three could be found that I knew something must have gone wrong . . .

"I called the police. I alerted the coastguards. What more could I have done?"

Roger seemed to be searching his conscience with ever-growing doubt.

Clare's face had grown progressively paler. Everyone else was embarrassed and, for some reason, uneasy. Only Mirabella seemed unmoved.

She had been sitting quietly, sewing. Now she looked up from her work. "That will do, Roger," she said firmly. "The tragedy happened. It has brought a lot of grief to a number of people—but it was nobody's fault."

"I just wanted Clare to understand," Roger muttered.

Clare looked at him. "But I do understand," she assured him. "I understand perfectly." And in the softly shaded light her face had something of the stark anguish of an Antigone.

"My dear boy, we *all* understand," said Sebastian.

Mirabella rapped with her thimble on a nearby tabletop. "Change the subject someone."

"We could talk about Dee," Michael suggested, turning from where he had been standing looking out at the moonlit garden. "I'm beginning to be a bit worried, for if she doesn't come this week I shall have gone. Then we may never meet."

"I'm looking forward to her coming too," said Clare valiantly. "She sounds such fun. Oh, it would have been nice to have found her at the cottage."

"When I arrived I thought she *was* there," said Antonia. "There were some of her things on the chest opposite the front door. A red leather belt, a pair of shoes, a wide silver bracelet, a half-eaten box of chocolates—and a newspaper two months old."

"Mrs. Epps at work, eh?" said Sebastian. "Lucky she's so honest. I never knew a girl as casual about presents as Dee."

"If you mean the silver bracelet," said Antonia, "Dee probably bought it herself. It wasn't expensive. A heavy chunky sort of thing with a weak fastening. There was a plain bit where an inscription could have been put—only there wasn't one, that's what makes me think it wasn't a present, men do tend to get sentimental about Dee."

"They do indeed," Sebastian agreed. "Clasped hands, pierced hearts, mysterious initials, and cryptic messages. Dee gets 'em all."

"A weak fastening," Beatrice echoed slowly. "I suppose that was why it was left at the cottage."

"From what I remember of Dee she was always losing things," Michael declared. "And not regretting their loss no matter who had given them to her. She had no use for sentiment."

"That's Dee all right," Sebastian agreed, "only grown into a charmer."

"And such a troublemaker," Mirabella turned to Clare. "You should have been here earlier. A scene of carnage and utter dis-astah!" She went on to give a spirited account of the scene at the dinner table.

When, at about ten o'clock, Antonia declared that she must go, there was a general move to see her home. Finally the five young people set off. Sebastian and his wife went with them to the edge of the woods.

Here Michael produced a torch, for it was dark with only a fitful gleam of moonlight falling across their path. Crossing the field Antonia, Clare, and Roger forged ahead, talking quietly and companionably. Michael and Beatrice fell back until their voices were only a murmur. An argumentative, almost quarrelsome, murmur, Antonia decided. She wondered what subject had aroused it.

They came to the lane.

"I've often wondered what the cottage looked like inside," Roger remarked.

"You must come in and see it," said Antonia.

"Perhaps Dee will be there," Michael suggested. Beatrice and he had caught up with the others.

"It's a picture-book cottage," Clare said. "Now, who would live there?"

"Red Riding Hood's grandmother," Roger declared promptly.

Michael made a sudden gesture for silence. "Looks as if the

wolf's there already," he muttered, indicating a darker shadow in the shadowy porch.

The shadow moved. Stepped into the moonlight. It was George Harker. He was a big, broad-shouldered man, handsomely grey-haired and impressive in a Savile Row suit.

Antonia introduced him to Clare and saw his expression change. "Keith's sister? This must be a sad occasion. Don't know when I've been so upset."

Clare's face glowed into life. "You were a friend of my brother's?"

"I like to think so. I have been down several times these last two months, staying at the Grand Hotel. That is how I came to know your brother—and his two friends. He was one of the most delightful boys I ever met. It would have given me great pleasure to have helped him to get a start in his chosen profession. Now that is no longer possible, but I would be honoured to help his sister in any way—any way at all—in this unhappy business."

Mentally Antonia shook a reproving head. Old world gallantry! No wonder he had not been able to hold Dee—not even with the added lure of the Maserati.

"Miss Hughes," George Harker had turned to her, "I apologise for calling so late but I must speak to you."

Roger plucked at her sleeve. "You said we could come in."

"It will have to be tomorrow," muttered Antonia, momentarily dazzled by the enchanting smile he had bestowed on her.

"I shall be dancing tomorrow morning," said Beatrice regretfully.

"Michael and I could come down in the morning, if that's all right by you, Antonia," said Clare. "We three could meet you here."

"Tomorrow then," Roger agreed. He said a general good night and set out on his lonely walk back to Treadle Bay.

Inside the cottage George Harker looked about the once-familiar room with a sad and downcast expression that touched Antonia's heart.

"Are you staying in Hone?" she asked when they were seated and her guest had refused the drink she had offered him.

He shook his head. "Staying at the Grand in Winstead. That's how I came to know Keith and his friends. Came down originally for a breath of sea air," he explained improbably. "Going back Monday." He paused, then added, "As a matter of fact I had something to tell Dee."

"I'm sorry she isn't here," Antonia answered. This was not strictly true. She felt that her friend's cheerful disinterest in everything that affected George Harker would hardly afford a panacea for his ills.

George sat staring silently into his hat for a moment. Then he said abruptly: "Fact is, my wife—Judith"—as if, Antonia thought, he had more than one—"been behaving strangely. Frightening really. Been following Dee about. Sometimes on foot, sometimes in her car."

Antonia nodded. "I know," she said soberly. "I've seen her several times. On Thursday she was having lunch in the same restaurant. It rather frightened me."

George glanced at her briefly. "Queer woman, Judith. Can't bear to be crossed. She's—implacable. That's the word for her. Implacable."

"You think she might try and harm Dee?"

"Succeed, too, I'd say."

Antonia recalled something Mrs. Harker had said earlier that evening. "How did you know that your wife had been following Dee?"

George looked shamefaced. "Been following her myself. Haven't spoken or anything like that." He sighed, then added: "Matter of fact, knew it would be no good."

Antonia nodded. She recalled something else that Mrs. Harker had said. It was that Dee had been in the cottage on Thursday, but this must be untrue. Where Dee had been there disorder reigned. Clothes left lying about, dirty dishes, newspapers strewn on the floor. "But, Mr. Harker—"

"Call me George," her guest said, in the strangled tones of extreme misery.

"But, George," Antonia amended, "if that's all you have to go on—"

"It wasn't all. Baratt, her groom, came to see me. He's been with her for years. Taught her to ride. When we married he came from Ireland to be with her. Her part of the marriage settlement she used to say."

"What did he tell you?"

"That Judith had been acting queerly. Had lost interest in everything. Didn't sleep. Sat for hours staring at nothing. When she decided to come down here he got anxious. No friends staying. No servants—not even Baratt. That's when he came to see me. The thought of her alone at the Limes frightened him. Frightens me too. What's she going to do there?"

"The trouble is that even when Dee gets here," said Antonia, "I don't see how we are going to make her take your wife seriously. She just laughs."

A spasm of pain crossed George Harker's hard-bitten face. "Dee does laugh, doesn't she? That was one of the things I loved about her. Judith now, she doesn't laugh much. Not unless she is angry. Baratt says he's heard her laughing quite a lot lately."

Antonia looked anxious. "What do you think your wife has in mind?"

"Not a subtle woman, Judith," George answered. "It would be something straightforward. Run Dee down with the car. Put her down a disused well—if she could find one. Throw her over the cliffs into the sea. Shut her up somewhere at the Limes."

Antonia stared at him with horror. "But why need it be anything?"

"Because," said George grimly, "Judith is like that."

When George Harker left Antonia stood at the front door listening to the sound of his footsteps getting fainter and fainter until they were lost in the distance. A moment later she heard the Maserati start up. It roared past the end of the lane. The hedge leapt into view. Momentarily a lacelike design of leaves appeared overhead. The car turned a corner. Plunged down the hill. The scene vanished. The sound died away. Antonia went in and shut the door. As she went up the stairs to bed the silence closed in on her, fold after fold, like a descending curtain.

She did not expect to sleep. Instead, worn out with the day's happenings, she dropped off almost as soon as her head touched the pillow.

A sudden crash of thunder woke her. Or so she thought.

She sat bolt upright, the last reverberation still sounding in her ears. The bedroom curtains were drawn back. The moonlight was pouring into the room. She waited, watching for a flash of lightning. Listening for another roll of thunder. Nothing happened.

Puzzled, she bent, peering at the face of her bedside clock. The time was half-past two. She had been asleep nearly three hours. There was not, she decided, any sign of a storm. So what had woken her up? The obvious answer came to her.

Dee had arrived.

Antonia scrambled out of bed, not troubling to put on the light. She pulled on her dressing gown and thrust her feet into her slippers. She opened the bedroom door, half-expecting to find the lights on in the sitting room and Dee smiling up at her from the foot of the stairs.

The place was in darkness. No sound of movement came from anywhere in the cottage nor from the lane outside. The whole place was utterly and entirely silent. And then, into that silence came a sound. A single metallic click. It came up quite clearly to Antonia's ears. She switched on the light and hurried down the polished treads, clutching the silk rope that took the place of banisters.

At the foot of the stairs she paused, looking about her. She could see nothing to account for the sound she had heard. Only the too-quiet room struck her as being undeniably sad; which last was purely imagination. The effect of her disappointment at finding the cottage empty.

"Dee!" she called experimentally. "Dee!" And the name returned to her mockingly, echoing softly. There was no other response.

She crossed the room to the kitchen, thinking that some pot or pan must have fallen from the walls. Only—wouldn't anything falling from a height make more than that single sharp click?

The kitchen was just as she had left it.

Obeying a sudden impulse she hurried up the stairs to Dee's bedroom. As she pushed open the door she became aware of a faint whisper of scent, not unpleasing. The personal odour of someone unknown. Then it was gone, dispersed by the draught blowing up the stairs.

Antonia stood there quite still. She was certain now that someone had been in the cottage. In this very room. Someone slyly cautious and unobtrusive. Departing silently except for the banging door.

She was conscious of an extraordinary feeling of unreality. She seemed in some curious way to be thinking with only the surface of her mind—and that quite sensibly. She went and looked out of the window, pressing her face to the glass. Staring out at the ancient ghostly apple trees below.

She went downstairs and opened the front door.

Hone was a very quiet place. Except for the occasional hoot of an owl or a belated car on the high road, there were no night sounds. The moon had come up over the downs and the countryside was as unreal as a backcloth on a stage. The dark clumps of bushes, the trees stiff as cardboard and just as still. The dusty lane looking like a stream of water flowing past the garden gate.

Antonia remembered how clearly she had heard George Harker's footsteps. It was even quieter now but there was no sound. Whoever had entered the cottage had made his escape.

She stepped back into the sitting room. The moonlight caught the edge of the chromium letter box. Almost absently she put her fingers through the opening, pushing back the flap. She removed her hand.

The flap fell, making exactly the same sound as she had heard while standing outside her bedroom door. Not much mystery there after all. Anyone, having let the front door slam, might well have crouched down, peering in through the letter box to see whether the noise had awakened the cottage's single occupant.

She could imagine the intruder, reassured, letting the flap snap back into place. And, treading on the grass verge, walking to the gate. Pausing there, he must have seen the light spring up in the cottage and, turning, have hurried away down the lane.

Antonia closed the door carefully and thoughtfully. Stood just inside the room. There was, she told herself, a natural corollary to what had taken place. It was that, whoever had entered the cottage must have done so by means of a key.

Walking cautiously, holding her breath, she crossed to where she had left her shoulder bag on top of the oak chest. She opened it and shook out the contents.

Her key, on its silver ring was there.

So it wasn't her key that was missing. It must have been Mrs. Epps's that had been taken. And by someone who had used it to rob the cottage.

She made a slow pilgrimage of the room. The two Staffordshire china dogs were still on the mantelpiece. The Chelsea porcelain figures still posed on the shelves of the bureau bookcase. The small silver knickknacks and bric-a-brac were still in the built-in corner cupboard. Neither the expensive record player nor her own transistor had been taken.

She went into the kitchen, aware of a deep reluctance for what she was about to do. She pulled open the drawer of the big kitchen table. In baize compartments the old-fashioned silver spoons and forks glinted up at her.

There had been no burglar.

All her fears returned overwhelming her. She had come to the end of her mental embargo. Must admit the dreadful insecurity of life. She bent forward, leaning against the kitchen table. She stared in front of her with fearful eyes. She felt sick.

Dee's key.

Whoever had let himself into the cottage had been no ordinary thief—*and he had had Dee's key.*

She had been gone since Thursday. What had happened to her in that time? Where was she? Wandering perhaps, robbed of her money and keys, lost and ill, along some lonely and unfamiliar road? Lying dead beside some woodland walk? Or buried in a shallow grave where no one would think of looking for her?

And those unknown eyes staring into the moonlit room? Now Antonia could admit their power to terrify. Suppose she had come down a few minutes earlier? Had crossed to the door? Bent to meet that evil gaze? Her heart shuddered at the thought.

What ought she to do, she wondered. Telephone the Winstead police? Tell them—what? That something had woken her up? That someone had been in the cottage? Had gone up to Dee's room? Had lifted the letter box flap and stared in?

Mentally she shook her head. It was all conjecture. To them unlikely conjectures at that. She decided that tomorrow she would consult Clare and Michael.

She went upstairs and crept into bed. When at last she fell asleep it was to have a disturbing and recurrent dream.

In it she was hurrying along a wide empty road which ran through a curiously dim and featureless landscape. Suddenly in the distance Dee appeared smiling. They hurried towards each other, hands outstretched and the nearer they approached the more shadowy Dee had become. As Antonia had been about to touch her she had vanished completely.

In her dream Antonia had hurried on, only to see Dee appear smiling on the horizon once more. The whole sad, strange sequence had been re-enacted.

Antonia had awakened to find her cheeks wet with tears. And, waking, was a prey to the deepest foreboding. Although she could not prove it she felt certain that something terrible had happened to her friend.

It was a feeling that was strengthened by the fact that there was no letter in the early post, no telephone call. No sign of Dee herself.

Antonia could settle to nothing. She made her bed and washed up the breakfast things. She hung about waiting for time to pass. She went into the garden and came in again, scared that the telephone might ring and she not hear it. Finally, she sat down in a chair and opened a book and forced herself to read, although afterwards she could not recall a single word.

Soon she heard footsteps coming down the garden path. She

looked out of the window and saw Michael. He was alone. She flung open the door. The smile with which he had been prepared to greet her faded. "Antonia, what's the matter? Have you had bad news of Dee?"

She shook her head. "No news," she said, gripping him by the arm. "But someone has her key. They used it to get in last night."

Michael's face hardened. He looked at her keenly. He listened to her story without a word. When she had come to the end he remarked soothingly, "Even if you're right and someone did get in last night, there is no need to think that he had Dee's key. It's easy enough to force that type of lock with a stiff bit of talc." He crossed the room and opened the door.

"Michael!"

"Yes?" He let go the door and turned. The door closed with a crash that shook the window frames. He hunched his shoulders against the noise. "I see what you mean," he admitted with a grimace. "The door certainly didn't do that when I was last here. It would have awakened anyone."

"And if you look, you'll see the lock can't be forced. The door opens inwards and fits into a frame. There's no space for a bit of talc. It's got to be a jemmy or a key."

Michael considered. "You don't leave a key hidden anywhere outside?"

"That's a country habit. Neither of us have adopted it."

"So that's out. Obviously you will have looked to see if your own key has gone. So—who else has one?"

"Mrs. Epps has a key. She comes in to clean."

"Well, then?"

Antonia shook her head. "Nothing has been stolen—and why else should someone have taken Mrs. Epps's key?"

"You don't think Dee herself—?"

"No—this was a man. The windows in Dee's bedroom haven't been opened since Mrs. Epps was here ten days ago—if then. The room was warm and close. As I opened the door it was just as if a man were there close to me. There was a faint, expensive scent, definitely male. It was dissipated in an instant —but it had been there."

"A smoker?"

"I don't know. I can't recall enough to break it down into its component parts."

"Then probably not a smoker. At least, not a heavy one. It's such a familiar smell and it does cling." He looked at her keenly. "Have you any suspicions as to who it might have been?"

She returned his glance with horrified eyes. "I did think that it might have been George Harker. That, when we found him in the porch last night, he was just going to let himself into the cottage."

Michael looked dubious. "Difficult to see what he could have wanted."

"It's difficult to see what anyone could have wanted," Antonia retorted. "But George Harker has run through the gamut of emotions since Dee broke with him. Desperation, fury, abject pleading—" She added in a low voice: "Sometimes he'd find out where she was and just stand staring at her. As if—as if he'd gone mad or something."

"Poor devil! Have you done anything about last night, such as telling the police?"

"That's the trouble. I rang up Hobday when I first arrived and found Dee wasn't here." Antonia went on to tell Michael the result of the enquiries made by the Winstead police.

"That settles it then. They won't do anything further. Not on the evidence you have now. Or rather the lack of it." Michael was silent a moment. His eyes were inscrutable. His lean face had an intent but shut-in look. "I think the only thing we can do," he said at last, "is to try and find out something more for ourselves."

"But how?"

"By making our own enquiries. Since someone saw Dee in Charing alone in her car, someone else may have seen her later—and not alone. She is so spectacular-looking that she is bound to have been noticed. That may give us a lead."

"That's a wonderful idea." A faint colour had returned to Antonia's cheeks. She added eagerly: "And when we've found out something more we can go to the police again."

Michael shook his head. "The police will only be interested

in a definite crime," he said with decision. "I fancy we shall have to get on without them for the time being." Antonia nodded her agreement. "That's settled then. Charing is about twenty-two miles from here. We'll motor there and then return very slowly stopping at any likely place to ask whether Dee had been seen. It's a pity today is Sunday. The pubs and garages will be open but possibly not with the same staff as on weekdays." He smiled at Antonia. "From what I remember of Dee she is hardly likely to have grown into a teashop addict."

"She despises them."

Michael nodded. He looked at his wristwatch. "It's now a quarter past eleven. I'll call for you at twelve o'clock. Unfortunately I left my new sports car in the parking yard at Hone Court and some fool backed his car into it. It's been at the garage in the village ever since. I was promised it back by three o'clock this afternoon. I don't suppose I can hire a car at such short notice this time of year, so if they can't let me have mine earlier we shall have to borrow Uncle Sebastian's. Anyway, you have something to eat and look out some good snaps of Dee— in her own clothes of course."

Antonia nodded. "I'll do that. I can't tell you what a relief it is to be going to do something definite. I felt sure that you or Clare would help me—" She broke off to add: "I'd quite forgotten. What has happened to her and Roger?"

"I meant to explain that. The fact is the third and last of those poor fellows came ashore early this morning. Roger has to go to Winstead to identify the body. Clare's still insisting on going with him to see her brother. When I left everyone was still arguing with everyone else."

Antonia shook her head sadly. "How dreadful for those two."

Michael smiled down at her. "Well, you aren't exactly having a ball. As for Clare, she must be what? Twenty-seven or -eight? Several years older than either Keith or Roger anyway. Old enough to know her own mind. Besides, I fancy that under that air of being half naiad there lurks a far stronger character than you imagine. So don't worry about her. Keep your thoughts on your own affairs. And don't fret about them either. We'll get some news of Dee. If not this afternoon then tomorrow."

Left alone Antonia felt more cheerful than at any time since she had arrived at the cottage to find it empty. She was even prepared to doubt the authenticity of her dream.

She went to a drawer of the bureau bookcase which she knew bulged with photographs of herself and of Dee—but mostly of Dee—taken over the past three years.

She selected half a dozen. Dee full face. Dee in profile. Dee smiling. Dee solemn. Dee in the Bug. Dee standing beside the Bug. She put the snaps into an envelope and the envelope into her shoulder bag.

She went upstairs and brushed her hair. She sat for a few minutes staring at her reflection but not really seeing it. In her mind's eye she was retracing the road from Charing to Hone. Thinking how many people there were on it to whom Dee had been known for years. In spite of the mist someone must have seen her. Spoken to her even.

And then there was Michael. He seemed so shrewd, so competent. So certain that something would come of their outing.

She hurried lightfooted down the stairs and into the kitchen. She made herself some coffee and some open sandwiches. She found herself whistling cheerfully as she moved about. Then, as there was not much time, she carried her plate and cup over to the table in the breakfast recess.

She switched on the light overhead and slid on to one of the long red leather seats. There she froze, staring. Her brief gaiety died. A cold hand seemed to close over her heart.

On the Formica tabletop, in Dee's handwriting, was a single word.

Vesuvian

FOUR

It was nearly eleven o'clock on Sunday morning when Septimus Finch arrived in Hone. The September morning was fine and sunny but the temperature had dropped and the wind blew in from the sea. He stopped his car where a waste piece of ground served as a car park and sat for a while gazing about him.

One or two shops were open and doing a brisk trade. There were several cafes in view, a Methodist chapel, and higher up the street the Bull's Head, an ancient inn enlarged into a somewhat pretentious-looking modern hotel. It was here that he had been able to book a room.

There were still plenty of visitors about. The voices of children came up from the beach. Seagulls wheeled overhead. Beyond the village the downs rose softly green against the sky and the minute bell from the unseen parish church fell softly on the thyme-scented air.

Finch found it difficult to imagine Dee Sumner in such pastoral surroundings. He wondered how she passed her time —or, rather, with whom?

He got out of his car. He took his suitcase and golf clubs and walked towards his hotel, a large lazy-looking man with an air of benign disinterestedness. He was hatless. His old tweed jacket was patched with leather. Above a sky-blue sweater his face loomed as disarmingly as that of a baby.

The reception clerk at the Bull's Head was loquacious. He told Finch that the lady whose room he was to occupy had left only that morning. She had cut short her stay because of their local tragedy. No doubt the gentleman had read of it?

He told him of Miss Vesey's arrival in Hone. Of the manager's deep regret that at the time he had not been able to offer her a bed. Of everyone's relief when it was learnt that the Chants of Hone Court had taken her in. They had known her brother and were a very hospitable family. Mr. Finch would be very welcome to watch the folk dancing there, if he were interested.

"Folk dancing?" Finch murmured. "Just fancy." He felt gratified. His curiosity about Dee Sumner had been satisfied on one point at least.

A chambermaid, used towels over her arm, was just coming out of the first-floor bedroom he was to occupy. He walked over to the window and looked out on the long straggling village street.

"I understand that Miss Sumner is down here?"

The reception clerk's expression changed. His glance was both sly and knowing. Mr. Finch was not their only guest looking forward to meeting their local celebrity. "She isn't here at the moment, sir, but she is expected."

Finch was disappointed. He had come down to play golf. The girl had been an added bonus. "I thought Thursday—" he murmured.

The reception clerk looked at him from under drooping eyelids. "The *other* lady in the case arrived at the Limes on Thursday. And Miss Hughes is at the Thatched Cottage. She got here yesterday." He almost giggled. "A delicate situation, wouldn't you say, sir? The two ladies being as it were but a stone's throw from each other."

Left alone Finch unpacked his suitcase and had a wash. So Ben had been wrong, he reflected. Mrs. Harker *had* returned to Hone. Had reached it on the day on which the girl who had

(*48*)

wrecked her life had been expected. For a moment he wondered whether there could have been a sinister connection between the two facts. He dismissed the idea. Antonia Hughes had arrived at the Thatched Cottage and seemingly had found nothing strange in her friend's non-arrival. Or had she? His curiosity was aroused.

He consulted his wristwatch. He was not meeting Ben until half-past two. There was plenty of time for him to call on the hospitable Chants. With any luck he might find Miss Hughes or Mrs. Harker there. He might even get an introduction to one or both of them. He went downstairs and asked the reception clerk the way to Hone Court. He got into his car and drove slowly out of the village and along the road which led to Winstead.

On the crest of the hill he saw the name, THE LIMES, painted on a white gate. He drove even more slowly. Not a blade of grass out of place. Not a curtain hanging askew by as much as an inch. Did this show a conventional nature? A rigid and unbending outlook? Such a woman would suffer more than most.

He saw the roof of what must be Dee Sumner's cottage since it was the only other house in view. He drove on.

Hone Court had a handsome pair of wrought-iron gates. And a notice that read that all were welcome to come in and watch the dancing. Finch drove slowly up the drive. There were fields to either side and some fine trees. Soon he was faced by a large sign. It read: STOP, VISITOR. PARK YOUR CAR HERE. "Here" being the lay-by carved from the wide grass verge.

Finch did as he was bid. He strolled on up the drive. Rounding a bend his gently ruminating gaze fell on an interesting scene.

An expensive, dark saloon car was drawing away from before the rosy brick façade of Hone Court. There were two people in it. A young man of glum but handsome appearance who was driving and a woman who, Finch judged, was a few years his senior. A woman of a strange Nordic fairness and an expression of desperate determination.

On a grass mound stood a short plump woman with

smoothly banded hair and a bright peasant-style frock. She stood on tiptoe, periwinkles growing about her feet, waving a small lace handkerchief after the departing car.

Over to her right on the lawn a dance was in progress to the music of an accordion. It was watched by a group of young spectators. The dance consisted of six men dressed in white with pads of bells fastened to their shins and carrying staves in their hands. Five of them were young and graceful. The sixth was a rotund elderly man. He was as active as anyone. Dancing here, prancing there, with shaking bells and clashing stave. Finch felt convinced he had never before seen so much energy displayed by one of his years.

The car vanished down the drive. The small figure stopped waving, not abruptly, but with a slow descending arm. A theatrical gesture that seemed to express farewell, despair, and resignation in equal parts.

She saw Finch and came towards him, the handkerchief still drooping from her left hand. Her right, with some nice rings on it, she held out to him in greeting.

"I am Mrs. Chant," she announced. "You have come to watch the dancing? You are very welcome."

"It is kind of you to say so. My name is Finch, Septimus Finch." He was glad to see that the name meant nothing to her. Murders and police court proceedings were not her reading. He thought too that he had seldom seen such bright and busy eyes. There would be little that escaped her sharp gaze.

"You dance, perhaps?"

"I used to—in Cornwall where my father is a solicitor." Since he hoped to see more of the Chants it was as well to establish a respectable background.

Mrs. Chant half-closed her protuberant eyes at him. "That delectable and myst-er-ious county," she said spinning out the adjective.

They were strolling towards the dancers. "You have a beautiful place here," Finch commented.

Mirabella Chant looked pleased. "It was built by a Chant from a design by Palladio. He pulled down the existing building. Now its successor is sadly in decay." Her voice fell a full octave. "We trust that it will last our time."

"You have no children to inherit?"

She shook her head. "It is perhaps a mistake for cousins to marry. Of course, we have a nephew, a dear boy. He says he does not want the property."

"He dislikes living in the country?"

Mirabella shook her head. "The reason remains a mystery. Can it be that he disapproved of the hereditary principle?" She did not wait for an answer but, abruptly discarding the grand manner, explained: "To be truthful we have never pursued the matter. So awkward to find Michael had changed his mind. We should then be forced to scrape and save to keep the property intact and in good repair." She added gaily: "As it is we have no one but ourselves to think of. Selfish perhaps but such a joy."

The dance ended. Sebastian Chant came across the grass mopping his face as he came.

"This is my husband," Mirabella introduced him, adding, "Isn't it nice to get a visitor so late in the season?"

"Septimus, eh?" said Sebastian in a deep rolling voice. "Don't tell me you're a seventh child."

"Not only a seventh child," Finch answered, "but a seventh son."

"And do you find that you have any supernatural gift?" Mirabella asked interestedly.

"None," said Finch sadly (it was the one thing no one at the Yard would allow), "unless you count an abnormal curiosity as a gift?"

"Curiosity?" Sebastian regarded him with his round-eyed, rather innocent stare. "Depends I'd say. Might be a vice. Even a curse." He turned to his wife. "Was that Roger's car?"

"Yes."

"Did Clare go with him?"

Mirabella nodded, her face taking on an anxious expression.

"The girl must still be in a state of shock." Sebastian turned to Finch. "You'll probably have read of our tragedy? How Clare Vescy's brother was drowned and his body carried on to the rocks. What you won't have read was that his face was terribly lacerated in the process. Now she insists on seeing him." He shook his head sadly. "Still, if Roger couldn't persuade her then no one could."

Beatrice Lynham came out of the house, running towards them. She was wearing another of her limp frocks. It had a frilled neck and a sash. A long gold chain encircled her plump neck. It hung almost to her waist and ended in an old-fashioned, pearl-studded gold locket.

"Sebastian," she called. "Come along. I'm dancing now. A square dance."

"Right!" Sebastian glanced at Finch. "You like to join in? It's what's called a Running Set. You'd soon get the hang of it."

"Mr. Finch tells me he *used* to dance," said Mirabella repressively.

Sebastian gave a roar of laughter. "Jealous, the poor creatures."

Beatrice was hanging on his arm. She turned to Mirabella, "We need another pipe of some sort for the music. Can I look in the Jumbo?"

"The Jumbo," Mirabella explained to Finch, "is a very big cupboard into which we put everything left behind at the end of the season. Every three or four years, when the cupboard is positively bursting at the seams with unclaimed goods, we clear it out and send the contents to the church bazaar." She appeared surprised to see Beatrice still waiting. "Why, Beatrice? Oh, the key! I do believe you asked me for the key." She detached it from a bunch dangling at her waist and gave it to the girl.

"I'll come with you, Beatrice," said Sebastian. "I fancy I've seen a three-holed whistle which should be just the thing." He paused, adding to his wife: "I forgot to tell you. Michael has borrowed the car for the afternoon. He and Antonia are going off on some project." His smile broadened. "I didn't like to ask him what."

Mirabella made a wide sweeping gesture. "What matters the project when one is young. Ah, youth, youth!" Her expression changed as she watched her husband and his companion walking towards the house. "Such a drearisome gairl. Don't you agree?" She went on: "Would you like to watch the next dance? Or will you come with me to the Home Farm?"

"I should like to come with you," said Finch promptly and truthfully.

They made an incongruous couple, the one short, plump, trotting along on small, high-arched feet. The other tall and sleepy-looking, strolling by her side with his deceptively lazy gait. Just before they plunged into the far woods Finch looked back. The dancers were forming up, but the red-haired girl and her companion were nowhere to be seen.

The woods were as neglected as the house. There was a great deal of undergrowth in which birds rustled and chirped. A rough track for lorries spoke of timber felling and a clear, swift stream, crossed by steppingstones, ran over a bed of sand and pebbles.

Finch told Mirabella how much he had admired one of her cottages. He described its position.

"The Thatched Cottage? Yes, it is attractive. But it no longer belongs to us. We sold it many years ago to some friends. Such a charming couple, both now, alas, dead. Their daughter still comes down quite often. So does the girl with whom she shares a flat in London. Such a dear child. So sensible."

This had been Finch's own reading of Antonia's character. At the time of the divorce she had been photographed several times arriving or leaving the court with her friend. An honest, intelligent face he had thought it.

"The two girls are at the cottage now?"

"Antonia is there. Dee, who owns the place, will arrive in her own good time."

They walked on. Finch would have liked to continue the conversation but Mirabella began to talk about the dancing.

She spoke with great emphasis, rolling syllables about as if they were cannon balls.

"In the early days man felt it was necessary to propitiate nature. He tried to identify himself with her wild creation . . .

(53)

"The peasants, contrary to general belief, were creators as well as transmitters . . .

"Ballet is another love of mine. I trained for it when I was young . . ."

They arrived at the Home Farm. Mirabella's reason for visiting it was to cancel the vast order for milk and eggs from the following Monday week, when the dancers would be gone and the season ended.

This done they began to retrace their steps. Finch had noticed several clearings from which trees and undergrowth had been removed. He enquired as to their purpose.

"In a very hot summer we use them for dancing," Mirabella answered. "It gives the lawn in front of the house a rest. And really the dances look even better against a truly sylvan background. Particularly when only a few people are participating."

She would have said more but for an unexpected interruption. There came a snapping of branches. Then into a small natural clearing some way ahead Beatrice came in sight through the trees, giggling and bounding fleetly through bracken and over hillocks.

A moment later Sebastian Chant appeared. Short arms flaying the air. Short legs going like pistons and his face an alarming shade of puce. The two of them disappeared into the trees and were lost to sight.

Finch stared after them with a fascinated eye.

Mirabella had come to a stop, listening to the fugitive sounds of flight and pursuit. "That hateful, hateful gairl," she said bitterly. "Always with an eye to the main chance. But if she thinks she will get anything out of Sebastian but chocolates and a few trinkets she is mistaken." She snorted contemptuously. "And if she comes to me trying to make mischief I shall laugh in her face."

She began to walk on quickly, with an agitated step. "To see her one would never think that Keith Vesey was her boy friend."

"She was supposed to be in love with him?"

Mirabella shrugged her plump shoulders. "Love? I only know that she was always at Treadle Bay Cottage. Forever attaching herself to Keith and his friend, Roger Frampton. Yes, whether they wanted her or not."

"I understood that Keith Vesey was something of a lady's man," Finch remarked untruthfully.

Mirabella looked surprised. "You must be thinking of Roger. He had immense charm. I suppose it is one of the ironies of life that we find now that he is in love with Keith's sister—and she certainly does not return his feelings."

"If he is so fascinating that must be difficult for him to accept."

"He exhibits every appearance of astonishment and incredulity," Mirabella rejoined twinkling.

"I suppose you knew both young men?"

"Yes, they were a brilliant couple. They were studying physics up at Oxford and were both expected to take first class honours. Keith was a late developer, quite content to stay quietly in Roger's shadow. But he was beginning to change, to become a personality in his own right." Mirabella smiled sadly. "He had a potential for greatness that only Roger appreciated. Roger, and just lately, myself."

By now they had emerged from the woods and were crossing the lawn. The dancers had gone. Their voices echoed cheerfully in the distance. From the sounds it was plain that a tennis match was in progress.

"Such energy," said Mirabella. "And to think that we let them off early this morning so that they could rest. They have had an unexpected invitation to give an exhibition of Folk Dancing in Winstead this evening." She added rather crossly, "All but that nasty, prying gairl. She prefers to hang round Sebastian—" She broke off, staring.

Antonia had appeared through the door leading from the dancers' car park. It was obvious that she had had a shock of some sort. Her face was colourless. There was a kind of horror reflected in her eyes.

Mirabella rose to the occasion in her own manner. With outstretched arms she sped towards Antonia on her ridiculously small feet. "Pale," she cried, "too, too pale." She enfolded the girl and pressed her to her bosom.

(55)

Antonia clung to her shaking. "It's Dee," she gasped. "I thought she hadn't been to the cottage but she had. She had."

Mirabella smoothed the dark hair. "Don't tremble so, my love," she crooned. Then she added briskly with one of her abrupt transitions of voice and manner: "Dee is a most unaccountable gairl. It is impossible to predict what she is going to do."

Antonia drew a long shuddering breath. "You don't understand. It's not that Dee came to the cottage and then left without letting me know. It's the way she did it." Adding under her breath so that Finch barely caught the words: "Or had it done for her."

Finch's recognition of the girl had been instantaneous. His thoughts raced. So, after all, Dee had arrived at Hone. Arrived—and then vanished. He wondered whether his own half-jesting warning to Ben Engleman was to be justified? Whether the formidable Mrs. Harker had been responsible? Whether it had been for the sake of revenge that she had braved the curiosity, the mockery and pity? Still, none of this explained Antonia's distraught appearance. What exactly was it she feared? He listened to what she was saying.

"I know I told you that Dee was coming down later. Actually she left London for here last Thursday. When I found that she hadn't arrived I thought—" Antonia remembered that a stranger was present and broke off abruptly, glancing doubtfully at Finch.

"You thought, as anyone who knew Dee would have thought, that, on the way down, she had met a personable young man and gone off with him," said Mirabella briskly. "That having been said, tell us why you now think differently?"

"You know what Dee is like in the house?"

Mirabella nodded. "Untidiest gairl in the world. Goes through the place like a high wind. Can't be in any room for ten minutes without leaving a trail of her possessions behind her."

"That's what's wrong now." Antonia's voice rose in a faint wail. "When I reached the cottage it was perfectly tidy. There was no sign that Dee had been there. There was no suitcase.

No car. Nothing in the larder. Nothing in the frig. There wasn't a crumb on the floor nor a single pot nor pan out of place. Yet, at some time, Dee *had* been there. I know that now."

Said Mirabella staring: "How do you know?"

Antonia explained about the word she had found written on the tabletop in the dining recess in the kitchen.

"But couldn't Dee have written it when she was down here before?" Mirabella asked.

"Last July? No, Vesuvian only came on the market a few weeks ago. I know because the man who did the publicity on it is a friend of mine."

"How most extraordinary," said Mirabella slowly, gazing darkly in front of her as if into a bleak future. After a moment's contemplation she said briskly, "We must go to the cottage at once and see what else is to be found. There must be something. Dee, for all her surface sophistication, is not duplicitous. She is no more capable of covering her tracks than the humble snail."

Said Antonia with a shudder: "I don't think she did cover them. Someone else must have done it for her."

Michael came hurrying from the house. "I saw you from the library window, Antonia," he explained. "What's wrong?"

They told him, Mirabella and Antonia in chorus. Finch said nothing. He looked only politely interested and very harmless.

Michael listened in silence. When the story was finished he said, "I'll get Uncle's car. I think it should start. I've been working on it for the last half hour."

"Why don't we use my car?" Finch suggested. "I left it round the corner of the drive."

"An excellent suggestion," Mirabella declared, introducing him to the other two.

"Do let us hurry," Antonia begged.

She got into the back seat with Michael. Mirabella sat in front. Finch had long held that he was one of Fortune's favourites. Now, as he accelerated down the drive, he reflected complacently that the present arrangement seemed to confirm this eminently satisfactory view.

When they reached the Thatched Cottage he manoeuvred

the car skilfully into the space in front of the garage. They all hurried towards the cottage.

Mirabella was the first in. She looked about her. Her face seemed to crumple. Turning she caught Antonia by the arm. "Dee can't have been here," she said tremulously. "She just can't. It's not possible."

Antonia stared back. "Are you like me? With a horrid creepy feeling that something terrible has happened to her?"

"There may be a perfectly ordinary explanation," said Michael sensibly. "And anyway, Antonia, you must have done some clearing up."

"Except for dusting my bedroom and washing the breakfast things I've done nothing," Antonia assured him.

Michael frowned. "No chance of Dee having gone off because of financial difficulties?"

"None at all. Dee's parents left her this cottage and quite a lot of money. And she was on the way to becoming a top model. She made a hit last winter when she looked so marvellous in all those Russian-style clothes. Great fur hats, high boots. That heavy embroidery—" Antonia's voice quivered to a halt.

"But suppose Dee only looked in and then went off?" Mirabella suggested hopefully.

"Without leaving me some sort of message?" Antonia asked. "She never has before."

"What sort of messages does she leave?" Michael asked curiously.

Antonia smiled wanly. "The last one read, 'Gone off with the dishiest creature. Back soon.'"

Back soon. Panic rose again in Antonia's breast. Where was Dee? What had happened to her?

"Let's see this mysterious word," Michael suggested.

They all went into the kitchen. Antonia switched on the light above the table. They all looked.

"Such a silly pretentious sort of name," Antonia murmured unhappily.

For the first time Finch was conscious of a distinct sense of foreboding. A disquiet, as if the single word had been both a farewell and a mute call for help. "Is Miss Sumner the sort of person who has to see a thing written before she can remember it?" he asked.

"Dee didn't write that on the table," Antonia explained. "She has a habit of tearing a strip off a newspaper and using any clear space for a shopping list or to remind herself of something. Then if there happens to be an advertisement on the other side or a photograph with a lot of printer's ink it acts as a carbon."

"And your friend had a newspaper with her when she left London?"

"She had the *Evening Standard.*"

"And where is it now?"

Antonia looked at him, desperately troubled. "I looked everywhere—even in the garden incinerator. It's gone—like Dee herself." Her eyes widened as she remembered the curious happenings of last night. She explained—not the dream—but what had, as she thought, taken place before the dream.

"You're certain it couldn't have been Miss Sumner returning for something?" Finch asked.

"Why should she wait until the small hours of the morning?" Antonia answered, indignant and surprised. "She owns this cottage. She doesn't need to peer through the letter box. And anyway secrecy isn't in Dee's nature."

Mirabella sighed unhappily. "It wasn't Dee who came in," she said positively. "It would have been out of character."

"It's all very mysterious," said Finch truthfully. "I can't help feeling one of you should tell the police."

"Yes, of course," said Antonia. "I suppose I ought to have done it instead of rushing round to Hone Court." She added with a certain bitter satisfaction: "This time P. C. Hobday won't be amused."

They went back into the sitting room. Mirabella sat down on the couch looking troubled, pursing and unpursing her lips. Finch chose a straight-backed chair looking about him with a guileless air. Listening to what Antonia was saying, while Michael watched her from the window.

Antonia replaced the receiver. "Hobday is coming," she said. "He wants us all to wait for him and meanwhile do nothing." She sighed abruptly. "That's going to be hard."

"When he's gone we could carry out our original plan," Michael suggested. "Go and look for some news of Dee."

Antonia shook her dark head. "It wouldn't be any good," she said sadly. "We know now that Dee was here. That she sat down in the kitchen and wrote Vesuvian on a bit of newspaper. And then what?"

"Someone came to the door," Mirabella suggested, wide eyed and staring. She gestured as if the unknown person still lurked outside.

"And when this caller left, Dee and all her belongings went with her." Antonia was shivering again. "There's something awfully—chilling about it. I mean—where was she when someone cleared up so expertly. I know she couldn't have done it herself even if she had wanted to." Another thought struck her. "That is odd. When we met yesterday evening Mrs. Harker spoke as if she knew that Dee had been here."

Michael looked at her quickly. "Judith had spoken to her?"

Antonia shook her head. "She didn't actually say that. Only that Dee was here."

Said Michael slowly: "That may just have been a bluff. An act put on to mislead us. To suggest that she had had nothing to do with Dee's disappearance."

"But how could Mrs. Harker have persuaded Dee to go with her?" Antonia asked.

"A gun is a persuader," said Michael. "Judith knows how to use one."

Mirabella clapped her plump hands together like cymbals. "Don't say such a thing," she cried, bouncing up and down on the couch. "Don't even think it."

Michael looked at her. "You believe it to be out of character?" he asked ironically.

"I don't! I don't!" Mirabella wailed. "That's the whole point."

Antonia shuddered. "Perhaps Dee is dead—and her murderer has her keys." She spoke clearly and bravely but her small face was pinched and pale. "But why should anyone kill her? And having killed her, what did they want here? It just doesn't make sense."

Finch had been standing silent and unobtrusive by the

chimney piece. Now he ambled forward. "We could find out something of what Miss Sumner did while she *was* here," he suggested.

Antonia looked doubtful. "I don't see how."

"Well," said Finch mildly, "what would your friend have done on arrival? Most people, I believe, develop some kind of routine."

Antonia nodded. "First of all she would have put the Bug— that's her car—into the garage. It isn't ever left in the lane because, as you saw, there isn't room for anything from the farm to pass. She'd come in here. Drop any parcels she had been carrying into that granny chair. Then she'd put down her suitcase, kick off her shoes and go over to the cellaret and pour herself a drink. She'd take it over to the couch and lie there propped up by all those cushions—" She broke off, her voice faltering. Her words had recalled Dee so vividly to mind that, for a moment, she seemed to see her, large, lazy, blond. Lying on her back, staring at the ceiling and wriggling her toes.

The cellaret was a handsome antique. Made of mahogany banded with ebony, it stood some three feet high, on four brass feet.

Finch walked around it. "A very nice piece," he murmured admiringly. "Late eighteenth century I suppose?"

"Open it if you want to," Antonia invited, a little surprised at this diversion. "It's rather nice inside. Lined with velvet. The original decanters and wineglasses are put away. Dee doesn't like to use them in case they get broken."

Finch went back to the fireplace. "Who, to your knowledge," he asked Antonia, "has been here, besides we who are here now?"

"Only George Harker. He is staying at the Grand Hotel in Winstead. He called yesterday evening." Antonia was undecided whether she should say anything more. She decided to keep it until Hobday arrived.

"And who had a drink from the cellaret—other than Miss Sumner?" Finch pursued.

"As far as I know, no one. I offered Michael a drink yesterday afternoon, and Mr. Harker one in the evening. Neither of them accepted, and I haven't had one. In the ordinary way I'm not madly keen." Antonia looked at the others. "I don't know how anyone else feels but I could do with a drink right now."

"Hardly a wise thing to do, is it? Suppose there were fingerprints," said Finch hurriedly.

"Of course," said Antonia, slightly taken aback at the thought. "We must wait."

"What time on Thursday would you have expected your friend to arrive?" Finch asked.

"If she came straight here she should have arrived by three o'clock. Even if she did some shopping on the way she should have been here by half-past."

"Would she remember to do the shopping?"

"Yes, she'd remember. Only she'd get carried away buying things we didn't really need. Then the essentials might be forgotten."

"If Miss Sumner got here by half-past three would she then have had afternoon tea?"

"That was the one meal she didn't care about."

"So when she sat down at that table in the kitchen it would have been to supper?"

"It would have been an evening meal of some sort. Dee never put on weight and she had a good appetite. Even if she were going out to dinner, about seven o'clock she'd go into the kitchen and eat several pieces of bread and something. Dripping or butter and honey. She wouldn't bother to cook for herself."

"So," said Michael, in the tone of one who saw, at long last, that they had established something useful, "at round about seven Dee was alone in the kitchen. Most probably alone in the cottage."

"Was she fond of her own company?" Finch asked.

"No, she couldn't bear it. Either she'd be just about to go out. Or she'd be expecting someone to arrive." Antonia's eyes widened in horror as she realised what her words had implied. She remembered something else. "Just before we left the restaurant where we had lunch last Thursday, Dee did say that she intended to go round to Hone Court as soon as she got here."

(62)

Mirabella shook her head. "She never came. She never even telephoned."

Said Antonia slowly: "I telephoned. Just before nine o'clock on Thursday evening. And again at a quarter past eleven. Each time I heard the bell ringing and ringing but Dee didn't answer."

So presumably whatever had happened had taken place before nine o'clock, Finch thought. He enquired whether Antonia knew any of Dee's men friends.

Antonia shook her head. "Not this sort of friend. Dee never brought anyone back to sleep even when she was alone. She thought that half the fun was going somewhere strange. Nothing would persuade her that it was dangerous."

Someone knocked on the front door. Roger Frampton stood outside. He looked pale under his tan and deadly tired. He stepped into the cottage. "So here you all are." He sounded reproachful. "I took Clare back to the Court but no one was there. I had to leave her alone." He looked about him. "What's going on? You look like a secret society."

"That's because I've discovered that Dee *has* been here," Antonia explained. "She seems to have disappeared."

"It did cross my mind that Miss Sumner might have joined those unfortunate young men in their dinghy," said Finch, looking mildly at Roger.

Roger laughed shortly. "Perhaps it was taking her on board that overturned the boat. But she wasn't in it when it put into Treadle Bay at half-past five. And there wasn't any talk of her having arrived when I nipped into the Bull's Head an hour later for a quick one with Michael and to book a table for eight o'clock dinner that evening."

"Unless Dee has changed very much since I knew her," said Michael, "that's an improbable solution. Dee was as sick as a dog the moment she got on the sea."

"Besides," said Mirabella reflectively, "three young men! What would Dee have done with *three* young men—and in a dinghy?"

Antonia looked at Finch. "Whatever made you think such a thing?" she asked wonderingly.

"When you have three high-spirited young men and a beautiful and susceptible young woman you do tend to wonder if they didn't get together. However," Finch added mildly, "I see it was a silly idea."

Antonia smiled at him. "Not silly," she assured him kindly. "Just unlikely."

Michael looked amused and slightly contemptuous. He changed the subject deliberately. "Did you identify poor old David?" he asked Roger.

Roger made a grimace. "Yes—but only just." He added in a conversational tone of voice that gave no one any suspicion of what was coming, "Did you know that fish nibble away the eyeballs and fingertips first?"

Mirabella paled. Antonia gasped and looked sick. Michael said, "My dear fellow!" in a tone of rebuke and Finch wondered what—apart from his recent ordeal—was upsetting the younger man.

Mirabella looked at Roger out of the corner of her eye. "How about Clare?"

"She didn't go into the mortuary after all," Roger answered in a curious flat tone of voice. "We met George Harker in Winstead. He persuaded her to let him take her place."

Mirabella's face brightened. "But that's splendid!"

Roger glanced at her briefly. "George Harker persuaded her quite easily. She wouldn't listen to me but Mr. Bloody Harker had no trouble." His voice was low and furious.

"I expect George caught Clare at the psychological moment," said Michael soothingly.

Antonia nodded agreement. "The nearer Clare got to the mortuary the more she must have shrunk from going in."

"It's because you're too close to her," Mirabella declared brightly. "Clare looks on you as a brother. And whoever heard of a sister taking any notice of a brother's advice?"

A spasm of pain twisted Roger's face. "I don't want to be a brother to her," he said roughly. He sank his handsome head into his hands. "I feel awful," he muttered.

Antonia was distressed. "I can't offer you a drink in case I smudge any fingerprints on the cellaret," she explained, "but

I could make everyone some coffee." As they seemed to like the idea she disappeared into the kitchen.

Finch looked at Michael. "So you think that Mrs. Harker holds Miss Sumner prisoner?"

Michael smiled grimly. "I hoped that as long as Antonia thought Mrs. Harker responsible she would believe that Dee was still alive."

"And your real opinion?"

Michael shrugged. "It still seems to me that Dee might have gone off of her own accord."

"Hear, hear," said Roger. He added with a shadow of his usual fascinating smile: "It's a queer thing but having been told not to touch anything I'm filled with a wild desire to rush around the room leaving fingerprints simply everywhere." No one encouraged this idea and he sank into his former gloom.

"There must be plenty of my fingerprints about," Michael remarked. "I used to know this room very well seven years ago. I picked up quite a lot of things that were once familiar to have a closer look at them."

Roger stared at him. "And who is going to look for these prints?"

Michael smiled briefly. "Hobday is coming."

Roger raised his eyebrows. "That I didn't know." He glanced through one of the windows. "And here he comes."

Michael opened the front door, Hobday entered. "Afternoon, ma'am. Afternoon, sir." He looked respectfully at the Yard man whom he had seen in Engleman's company and gave him an impressive "afternoon, sir" all to himself, at which Michael looked at Finch with a new and sudden interest.

"Miss Antonia not here?" Hobday asked.

"I'm just coming," Antonia cried, opening the kitchen door. She smiled at the Constable over the tray she was carrying. "I've put an extra cup for you. And I've brought some sandwiches for the others."

"Thank you, miss. A cup of coffee will be very nice." Hobday smiled his comfortable smile. "I telephone Winstead before I left," he went on. "The Inspector should be on his way now."

Mirabella's head jerked up. An expression of profound alarm crossed her face. "Not Inspector Engleman?"

"No need for you to fret, ma'am. Happen you won't have to see him after this once," said Hobday.

"Don't you think—" Mirabella had lowered her voice. She looked round furtively as if she feared that the Inspector might already have managed in some way to get into the room. "Don't you think that I could just slip away before the Inspector arrives?"

Hobday shook his head. "He'd only wonder what you'd been up to, ma'am." His gaze, like his speech, was remarkably tolerant.

Michael's sober face relaxed, the skin crinkling into lines of amusement about his eyes. "Now what have you been up to, Aunt?"

Mirabella drew herself up. "You disrespectful boy. Now indeed! It was only once. And then I did it for the best."

"Did what?" Roger asked.

"It was two years ago," Mirabella explained. "I had had some jewellery stolen. The Inspector had the audacity to declare that our parlourmaid, such a nice gairl, was implicated. He insisted that his sergeant was right. That she had unlocked the back door and let the burglar in."

"And had she?" Antonia asked perching, cup in hand, on the arm of the couch.

"She admitted it in the end." Mirabella drew herself up and added unreasonably and with considerable hauteur: "I cannot help feeling that Inspector Engleman should have accepted my word in the first place." Her tone of voice implied that she found his failure to do so both vulgar and despicable.

FIVE

Detective Inspector Engleman was six feet tall and held himself well. He had blue eyes, a small bristling moustache and the complexion that so often goes with sandy hair, red, rough, and looking as if the sun had caught it. Usually a cheerful man he couldn't help a slight look of aversion crossing his face when he saw Mirabella Chant.

She too was not unaffected. "Good afternoon, Inspector." Out of a guilty conscience her eyelids flickered and she spoke in a high arch voice. As if, Finch reflected amused, she and Engleman had once been lovers. "I don't think you know anyone here—except myself, so let me introduce you. This is Miss Hughes, Mr. Finch, my nephew Michael Chant, and Mr. Frampton."

Engleman bowed. "I know Mr. Finch."

Mirabella looked at him suspiciously. Had he meant that in a derogatory sense? Was he thinking that Mr. Finch's reason for coming to Hone was connected in some way with Dee's disappearance?

"Mr. Finch arrived here only this morning to see the folk dancing," she said firmly, and her somewhat bulging eyes were watchful. "He used to dance himself in Cornwall—the Flora or Furry Dance of Helston, you know."

"Indeed?" Engleman had produced a notebook and was staring at a blank page with an equally blank expression.

Mirabella was determined to distract the Inspector's mind from what she felt might well be an unfriendly approach to her new-found friend. "The dance is said to have been a device to frighten away the devil. According to the legend he was threatening the town in the form of a dragon when he espied the inhabitants forming their own dragon, as it were, which quite upset him." She smiled expansively at Finch. "No doubt you know the story?"

Finch nodded. He stood, large, amiable, and not at all put out, one elbow resting on the high chimney piece. "As I remember it the devil swerved away from Helston. Fell into Looe Pool and vanished in a cloud of steam."

"Exactly," Mirabella cried, delighted at this corroboration on Finch's part. "The dragon myth is often associated with a river given to overflowing its banks—" She caught sight of Antonia's pale face and strained expression. "My dear child! Do forgive me. I let myself be quite carried away by my enthusiasm." She drew herself up. "Now, Inspector, let us proceed."

"I was going to explain," said Engleman, "that, in ordinary circumstances, the police would not be able to begin a search for Miss Sumner as early as this, since she is of age and a free agent. However, according to Hobday, there are some unusual circumstances which may well override such considerations."

"Oh, there are," Antonia cried with anxious eagerness. "We all thought that. We came back here and talked things over. And the more we talked the more mysterious Dee's disappearance seemed."

Antonia went on to describe the course of events, from Mrs. Harker's strange behaviour in London to where she, Antonia, had rung up P. C. Hobday for the second time.

Engleman listened intently. There were one or two unusual points to her story but none that was inexplicable. Still, the matter would have to be investigated. He said aloud: "I think we must search this cottage, if you would be kind enough to

(68)

leave it to us for a time. Also we must look for any strange fingerprints, which means that we shall need to take all yours so that we shall know which to eliminate. Then if Miss Hughes would return in say"—he consulted his wristwatch—"two hours' time we may have some good news of Miss Sumner."

"You had better all come back with me," said Mirabella rising thankfully to her feet. "It seems a very long time since we had those sandwiches. I, for one, feel quite famished. There're the dancers too. We may be in time to see them off." She turned to Engleman. Their meeting had gone better than she had imagined possible. "An unexpected invitation to dance at Winstead," she explained. "An open air performance. Music by the Go-Go Guitarists. Only a trio but quite inspired. Good-bye, Inspector. Such an anxious time for us all."

"You'll stay, please, Mr. Finch," said Engleman briefly.

Mirabella's suspicions returned. "Mr. Finch, one moment." She beckoned, led him a little way along the garden path. "Stand up to the Inspector," she counselled him, patting his sleeve and looking anxiously up into his face. "Don't be nasty. Just rather reserved." She nodded, smiled encouragingly and hurried to join the others who were waiting for her in the lane.

Finch was touched. He concluded rightly that Mirabella considered that their shared experience in the woods constituted a bond between them. He went back into the cottage. McKnight, he found, had produced his fingerprint kit. Assisted by Hobday he was already at work on the cellaret.

Engleman looked at Finch with amused eyes. He was sorry that he could not rib him on his dancing prowess. Obviously, since Finch was his superior, it would not do in front of Sergeant McKnight and the Hone constable.

"While McKnight is busy we may as well have a look at this mysterious word," he remarked. He led the way into the kitchen and closed the door. "So we have become victims of one of your famous hunches. I can't say I'm impressed."

"You don't find something a bit ominous in this girl's disappearance?"

Engleman shrugged. "Miss Sumner is too fond of her own way. Her friend suffers from an anxiety state."

"At least that isn't your complaint, Ben," said Finch in his soft drawl.

Engleman turned to look at the facsimile of the word written on the tabletop. "You must admit that Miss Sumner could have been responsible for everything that has taken place—even to coming back secretly last night for something she had forgotten? That is, if she had some reason for wanting to disappear for a time."

"There is one thing that, to my mind, would suggest some form of criminal activity. One in which Dee Sumner had no part."

"You mean the possibility of a stranger's fingerprints appearing on the cellaret? That may prove useful in the future. It proves nothing now."

"I mean," said Finch slowly, "the probability that there are no fingerprints at all on the cellaret."

Engleman's red face grew redder. "Damn and blast," he said under his breath. "I might have known that you'd have something like this up your sleeve."

Finch grinned. "It was not for nothing that my nose fell a-bleeding on Black Monday."

For some obscure reason, the quotation seemed to remind Engleman of something. "If this business does turn out to be serious there is one thing you can do for me."

"Delighted, dear boy."

"Then keep Mrs. Chant out of my hair."

Finch nodded. "I gathered that you had behaved towards her in an ungentlemanly way," he said solemnly.

"Lor' save us!" cried Engleman. "What has that woman been telling you? When I think of what she did. The misleading statements she made. The false evidence she planted. Why, the sergeant in charge nearly went bonkers. I wanted her prosecuted but the Chief Constable wouldn't have it. And he was right. I can see that now. If the story had ever got out we should have been the laughingstock of the county."

In the sitting room McKnight, with a camel's-hair brush and a mixture of chalk and mercury, was bringing up some fingerprints on the gate-leg dining table.

"That's a rum go, sir," he said, on seeing Engleman. "There's not a single print on that cellaret. Not even on the bottles of liquor, although they've all been used and two of them are three parts empty. Seems as if someone has been polishing them—and that's not natural however you look at it."

A silence followed on his words. A strangely uneasy silence. All saw, with varying degrees of clarity, that the nature of the enquiry had changed.

McKnight and Hobday returned to their task.

"There's still no proof that Miss Sumner is dead," Engleman declared doggedly.

Finch looked at him. "My dear Ben, why else should anyone have wanted to make it look as if she had never been here? And you must admit there are several likely candidates for the part of murderer."

"You name them."

"There's George Harker. He may have killed her in a fit of frustrated passion."

Engleman stared. "*George* Harker?"

"At the moment he's staying at the Grand in Winstead. He may have come, as he said, to warn Miss Sumner. On the other hand he may just be haunting the scene of his crime."

Engleman snorted. "One snag to the theory of George Harker as a murderer is that Miss Sumner doesn't sound as if she'd frustrate anyone. From what I hear she is a soft touch and an easy lay."

"But not to George. When Miss Sumner was through she was through."

"I would have thought Judith Harker a more likely claimant for the part of killer."

Finch shook his head. "Mrs. Harker doesn't want the girl dead. She merely wants her to wish herself dead. No, if Mrs. Harker is responsible for the disappearance, the girl is, bar accidents, still alive."

"Alive?" Engleman echoed incredulously. "How would Mrs. Harker have got the girl to go with her?"

"It wouldn't have been difficult. Dee Sumner was a good-natured girl. Mrs. Harker had only to spin her a well-thought-out yarn."

"Such as?"

"She might have said that George was at the Limes. That he was willing to go back to his wife, if he could hear from Dee's own lips that she had finished with him."

Engleman, rallying, shook his head with a look of mock wonder. "The things you dream up, Septimus. Any more theories?"

"That Miss Sumner on her way down was unfortunate enough to pick up a sex maniac, a pervert, a sadist. A man with a kink of some sort—and bring him back here."

Engleman's face darkened. "Now there I am with you. Every week almost somewhere in England some girl is murdered, either because she hitched a lift in a strange car, or because she gave a stranger a lift in hers. These things are reported in the newspapers yet they go on taking place." He was watching his sergeant at work. "But in this case I feel that Miss Sumner is likely to be pretty annoyed if we begin a full-scale search for her body and then she turns up—" He broke off to enquire irritably: "McKnight, what on earth are you doing crawling about on the floor?"

The sergeant got to his feet. His expression was troubled. "What fingerprints there are, sir, belong to Miss Hughes, young Mr. Chant and his aunt. There are no others." McKnight hesitated. Then he burst out: "It's a queer thing, sir, but upstairs, when I was getting Miss Sumner's fingerprints so that I could compare them with any found elsewhere, I noticed a slight film of dust over everything as was only to be expected since it's ten days ago since the cleaning woman was here. In this room there isn't a speck to be seen."

"Miss Hughes says she hasn't done any dusting," Finch murmured.

"Is that so, sir?" said Engleman. "Then someone else has. Every surface liable to take a print has been—well, one could say, almost polished. Couch legs, windowsills, radiators, the record player, bottles."

"But that doesn't make sense," Engleman cried. He realised,

(72)

even as he spoke, that, in rather a horrible way, it did have significance.

McKnight proceeded to spell it out. "It occurred to me," he said slowly, "that someone might have had a brainstorm in here. And that, when it was over, he couldn't remember what he had touched." He added uncomfortably: "God knows what else he did when he wasn't himself, as you might say."

Everyone, for a moment, was appalled. It had been difficult up to now to believe that anything violent or sinister had happened in this pleasant, charming room. There was no sign of disorder. No ominous stains, no indication of a struggle. Yet now it seemed to the four men that a golden-haired girl, who had once been beautiful, lay still and blindly staring from an obscure corner of the room. While a shadowy figure worked with desperate efficiency to make it appear that neither of them had been in the cottage that fatal evening.

"And that," Finch declared sadly, "is not a nice picture. Not nice at all."

McKnight went off to look over the rest of the cottage for fingerprints. Hobday, his face wan and sick, trudged after him, carrying the sergeant's fingerprint kit in its grey plastic box.

Left alone Finch and Engleman began to search for any sign of the murder they now suspected. They searched silently and skilfully. Twenty minutes later they had to admit that they had failed.

"But not even a bread crumb," Finch lamented. "Not in the larder. Not in the kitchen. It doesn't seem natural."

"Girls today don't eat bread," said Engleman wearily.

"This one did—and in quite large quantities." Finch sank into one of the deep armchairs. "Well, at least, thanks to Antonia Hughes, we can piece together some of the things that happened last Thursday afternoon up to the time of the crime. Dee Sumner probably got here between three o'clock and half-past. She either brought someone with her or a visitor arrived shortly afterwards." Finch explained how he had reached this conclusion.

"We know that she was alive round about seven when she was accustomed to have a snack in the kitchen. By this time

(73)

her companion must have gone. Otherwise he would have joined her in her meal. And, being the careful fellow we know him to be, would have noticed the word written on the table-top.

"Now it's unlikely that Miss Sumner went out to keep an appointment with her late companion. Her car was well known in the district. In spite of the mist, still not very thick, some-one would have recognised it. The news that she was down here would have got around. Reached Hobday or Miss Hughes.

"So what happened? Was it a second person who called after supper? It is unlikely but possible. Or was it the same man? Was he now in a strange frightening mood? Did Miss Sumner realise that he was not normal? Did she tell him to go? Try to resist him?"

Said Engleman again: "We don't actually *know* that murder was done."

"And yet what other explanation can there be? After all, it would have been safe enough. There are no other houses near. No one would have heard if she had screamed. And we do know that when Miss Hughes telephoned from London at about nine o'clock, there was no answer. That when she tried again at a quarter past eleven, there was still no reply."

Finch fell silent, held for a moment by the strangeness of the picture his words had conjured up.

"And this man?" he continued at last. "Why did he leave at all? Was he expected somewhere for dinner? Had he a wife and children waiting for him? Had he an evening job? We don't know. All we can say for certain is that he is not a local resi-dent."

"How d'you make that out?" Engleman was looking at the photographs on the drawer of the bureau bookcase. It seemed impossible that any one as lovely and vital-looking as Dcc Sum-ner could be dead.

"Because his one idea has been to make it appear that Miss Sumner never got here. And that suggests two things. That he was someone who already knew of her reputation. And that in a few days' time he would have left the district. Left it long before Miss Hughes's anxiety had grown strong

(74)

enough for her to have reported her friend to the police as missing."

Engleman turned. "He may already have gone."

"I thought that—until I heard Miss Hughes's story of having been disturbed last night."

Said Engleman slowly: "Then whoever was here must have come in consequence of something said yesterday, either at Hone Court. Or later when George Harker was here talking to Miss Hughes."

Finch nodded. "Yes, the connection must be there. And that narrows our field of enquiry. Was our killer indeed George Harker? Was he one of those two attractive dark young men? Michael Chant, who may once have been the girl's lover, in spite of the fact that she was below the age of consent? Or was it Roger Frampton, made surly and dangerous as a starving animal by his need for Clare Vesey?"

"Might even have been Sebastian Chant. He's always fooling about with some girl or other, so I'm told."

Finch looked doubtful. "I should imagine that is just a kind of pride in his virility on the part of the old boy. He doesn't fly high. Besides he's known Miss Sumner all her life. He's not likely to conceive a sudden passion for her."

Engleman produced his notebook. "Anyway, it's an angle that must be looked into." He wrote, muttering aloud, "Has anyone concerned got a record for this sort of thing—or even a reputation?" He returned his notebook to his pocket. "I'll get back and report to the Superintendent. But first I'll telephone Hone Court and suggest that Miss Hughes doesn't return here just yet. We can have a second search using the proper equipment. There must be something—if it's only a single hair."

"There's the car, too, to find."

Engleman nodded. "I haven't forgotten it. I fancy it won't be in the woods. Woods in summer and in the weather we've been having mean children and courting couples. Someone woud have seen it. No, a disused quarry, the garden of an empty house or a tumble-down barn seem the most likely places."

"Since our man was banking on getting away before any

(75)

worthwhile enquiry was instigated my guess is that you'll find the car somewhere quite obvious. Obvious—but where its presence won't attract any attention."

McKnight and Hobday reappeared. The former announced that the only places which had been cleared of all fingerprints were the sitting room and the toilet. This last, with a bathroom, had been built out at the back on the ground floor. "And he's polished all the shoes in Miss Sumner's bedroom. A whole cupboard of 'em. He's a nutter all right."

Engleman still had a faint, unexpressed hope that the whole grisly picture of murder was just a figment of his friend's too lively imagination. But to be on the safe side, in case the intruder of the previous night really existed—in case he had not found what he was looking for—Engleman left McKnight at the cottage. He could preside over a second, more wide-spread search. And when he left a constable would remain behind.

Finch walked with Engleman to the lane. "We'll meet again," he said amiably.

Engleman looked at him. "Since Superintendent Bollard was rash enough to say that you can make a few discreet enquiries if you like we're perfectly certain to meet again—by some open grave, no doubt."

"Harsh words from my old and trusted friend," said Finch sadly. "I am deeply hurt."

Finch took a slightly cynical view of the show of tolerance on the Superintendent's part. However, he intended to take full advantage of it. His first move was to ask Hobday where he would find Mrs. Epps. This done he reversed his car back into the main road and drove into Hone for a quick belated snack before setting out on his quest.

The Epps family lived in an old flint cottage crouched under a hump of the downs. Tom Epps leant upon the gate. He was a heavily built young man. He had a sly but amiable expression.

When Finch laid a hand on the gate he moved aside. He made no answer to the detective's greeting. Only when he had passed he shouted after him, "Mind the Spaniards."

(76)

The cottage door opened. Mrs. Epps appeared. She was a small, neat woman with a pleasant expression and an air of bustling competence.

"Hope Tom didn't startle you, sir," she said. "He's a good boy. He doesn't mean any harm."

"But what has he got against the Spaniards?"

"It was when he was still at school and heard tell of the Spanish Armada. I don't know why, I'm sure, but somehow it stuck in his mind that all Spaniards were dangerous. Sometimes he calls out that nonsense but no one takes any notice." Mrs. Epps looked enquiringly at her visitor. "Were you wanting Mr. Epps? He's out at the moment."

Finch produced his warrant card. "If I might come in?"

Mrs. Epps looked first startled, then apprehensive. "It's not Tom, sir, is it? He never does no harm." She opened the door into the parlour. A room shiningly clean but shadowy from the number of pot plants standing on the windowsill.

Finch shook his head. "It's nothing to do with your son."

"Then it's Miss Dee," Mrs. Epps declared as she closed the door. "I've always been afraid for her, carrying on as she does. And not a bit of harm in her, sir."

"Have you seen her lately?"

"Not since she was here in July." Mrs. Epps was staring at him with troubled eyes.

"What I'm going to tell you is, for the moment, in confidence. We don't want needless talk and scandal. The truth is that Miss Sumner arrived at the Thatched Cottage last Thursday. As far as we know she hasn't been seen since—and everything she brought with her, including her car, has disappeared."

Mrs. Epps put her hand to her heart. It was an instinctive, oddly moving gesture. "God help us," she said, "that poor, dear girl."

The telephone rang in the hall.

"Now who can that be?" Mrs. Epps demanded. She left the room. A moment later she was back. The last of the fresh colour had gone from her face. She said almost fearfully: "It's Mr. Hobday—for you."

Finch nodded. Was it news of Dee? Dee dead? All that sexy

loveliness lost and gone? He took up the receiver. "Finch here."

"Glad I caught you, sir," said Hobday's voice. It added on a warning note, "For all it's a party line and none too private."

"I understand."

The slow country voice ran on. "I've a message for you, sir, from Superintendent Bollard. He'd be glad if you'd meet him at the Limes. I'm on my way there now."

"Thanks. I'll be along." So that's it, Finch thought. Only the worst sort of news would bring the Superintendent out. He replaced the receiver. He went back to the parlour. "I don't know what this is about, Mrs. Epps, but I have to be off. Meanwhile, I'd be glad if you'd ask around whether anyone has seen Miss Dee or her car. It should sound natural enough since she is expected about now."

Mrs. Epps stared at him blindly. "D'you think it can be news of Miss Dee?"

"We must hope not," Finch answered soberly, "for if it is it can only be bad news."

As she opened the front door he roused himself from his rather painful thoughts to enquire whether Treadle Bay Cottage was in the next dip of the downs.

"That's right, sir," Mrs. Epps agreed. "It was built originally for a shepherd when there was a lot of sheep grazing here. It's been let to visitors for a good many years now. Mr. Frampton and his friend came there in June."

Tom was still in the garden. "I seen 'un," he cried. "Walking and crying out—"

"Give over, Tom, do," said his mother cutting him short. "That poor young gentleman! I went round yesterday to see if I could do ought to help. It took me over an hour just to wash the dirty dishes. You never saw such a state as the kitchen was in. But there, it was Mr. Vesey who was the handy one about the place. Mr. Frampton must be fair lost without him."

Tom had fallen silent, scowling. As Finch let himself out of the garden gate he shouted after him, "Mind the Spaniards," and broke into roars of mindless laughter.

SIX

Roger's car, bearing the party from the Thatched Cottage, swept round the last bend of the drive. It came to a halt on the gravel sweep. Except for the cawing of rooks in the elms there seemed an unaccustomed silence about the place.

The only person in view was Sebastian Chant. He stood on the lawn a rather disconsolate-looking figure. His shoulders were hunched. His hands were thrust deep into the pockets of his shorts.

"You've missed the gang," he called. "They left about half an hour ago. Don't know what difference they think they'll find but they wanted to bathe in Winstead." He came towards them as he spoke, petulantly kicking up the gravel in front of him.

"We've been looking for Dee," Mirabella told him, getting out of the car. "Such a mystery. We know now that she arrived at the cottage on Thursday because she wrote Vesuvian on the kitchen table."

Sebastian was unimpressed. "Why should she do a damn' fool thing like that?" he demanded in a kind of angry reason-ableness. "My father used to call matches Vesuvians. Burnt like fireworks I remember. Wouldn't have thought Dee would even have known the name let alone go around writing it down."

Mirabella's bright expression faded. "Don't try and explain," she advised the others. "I know that tone. Sebastian's put out about something." She led the way into their own wing of the house, adding hopefully, "Perhaps he has quarrelled with that nasty gairl."

She glanced at the grandfather clock. "Twenty-five minutes to four. What a nice time. It means you can have an early tea or a late luncheon. Or, like me, a combination of both."

In the old-fashioned larder, on slate shelves, was the plenteous food to which she had been looking forward. Her visitors were urged to take what they fancied and carry it into the kitchen cum dining room.

There followed a bustle and the sound of cheerful voices. Every one felt relief at having left the obscure, rather frightening and certainly Dee-ridden atmosphere of the Thatched Cottage.

"What do you think the Inspector meant when he said that he knew Mr. Finch?" Mirabella asked presently. She was eating one of the beef sandwiches cut for her by Michael.

"I noticed that he was very careful not to look amused when you were talking about the Furry Dance," Roger remarked, putting sweet pickle on the top of his sandwich.

"While Sergeant McKnight looked positively scandalized," said Michael.

"Scandalized?" Mirabella echoed.

"As if, my dear aunt, you had committed *lèse-majesté*," Michael explained with a grin.

Mirabella chewed reflectively for a moment. "What you are both saying is that you think he's a policeman."

"Some sort of policeman," Michael corrected. "Superior to Inspector Engleman anyway."

"You mean MI5 or something like that?" Roger asked doubtfully. "Can't say he looks it."

"A pose, my dear fellow," said Michael cheerfully. "Although I didn't realise it at the time, I can see now that he got a remarkable amount of information out of Antonia in a very short time. Yes, I'd say he was a police officer. What do you think, Antonia?"

"I think I've seen him somewhere before," Antonia answered thoughtfully. "Only I can't remember where."

Mirabella glanced out of the window. "There's Clare." Adding, conscience-stricken: "I do hope she has had something to eat. I quite forgot to tell her to help herself, if no one was around."

Roger followed the direction of her gaze. His face darkened. "What's that fellow doing here?"

"George Harker? I expect he came to tell Clare how he got on," said Mirabella. "After all, she did give him a commission." She pushed up the window. "Hullo, you two!" she cried smiling and waving a sandwich at them. "Have you had anything to eat?"

Clare nodded. "George has just brought me back," she called.

"Come in, both of you."

Clare looked across at Mirabella, shading her eyes from the sun's rays with her hand. "George is just going but I shall be in."

Mirabella nodded. "You do that," she called. She shut the window. "At least Clare knows her own mind. And, it seems, George's mind as well." She spoke rather tartly. Clare, whom she had welcomed into the house as a dove with a broken wing, was, she considered, beginning to show signs of a dominant nature and that she did not like. "Imperatorial," she murmured aloud, savouring the word. She caught Michael's amused gaze. "Give Antonia some more meat," she ordered. "Girls these days have far too many meals in restaurants."

The door opened and Clare came in. She came in very quietly. She seated herself in one neat movement, resting her lightly linked hands on the table in front of her.

Roger said nothing.

Michael said, "Have some homemade cider?" And then, as he filled a glass for her: "I should have said that George Harker was the last sort of man you would have liked, Clare."

"It must be the attraction of opposites," said Clare thoughtfully. "The George Harkers of this world bestride the universe with an ease that we unpractical folk never attain."

"And that appeals to you?" Roger persisted.

"I find George's predictability restful," Clare admitted. "For instance, I might dream for years of the golden apples of the Hesperides. But mention it to George and he'd go straight off to Harrods and order one."

They both laughed. She looked at Roger and her mirth died.

It was then that, watching the two dark faces intent on Clare's fair one, a truly terrifying idea came to Antonia. It was one that had already occurred to the police. The suspicion that either Michael or Roger might have been responsible for Dee's disappearance.

Neither of them, it was true, looked a monster but then many murderers didn't look like monsters. In fact, if Dee were to be believed, many of them had been good-looking—and fascinating. She could not recall any of their names but Dee had once reeled off a long list—all handsome and all monsters.

She could not but see how easy it would have been for either Roger or Michael to have got off with Dee. And, while Roger was attractive to everyone, it was Michael whose name had been linked with that of her friend in the past.

"He has always had an eye for a pretty girl. You should have seen him with Dee in the old days . . ."

She recalled how Michael had alluded to Dee as spectacular-looking. Had that been because of what he remembered? Photographs he had seen? Or because they had met recently?

She felt the horror of suspicion chilling her blood and hollowing her stomach. The thought came to her that, before suspecting the two men, she should make certain that Dee was not imprisoned at the Limes as George Harker had hinted. Suppose she were there. Alive, well—

She became aware of Michael's voice speaking to her. "Are you all right, Antonia?"

"She does look queer," said Roger.

"She is going to faint." Clare sprang up and began to chafe her hands. "Put your head between your knees," she advised. "You'll feel better then."

(82)

"Michael, fetch the brandy," said Mirabella.

Their voices sounded to Antonia loud but far away and indistinct. They were like the beating of birds' wings about her head.

"I'm perfectly all right," she said stiffly. She drank the generous measure of brandy because it seemed less trouble to do so than to refuse. "I keep thinking of Dee," she explained, getting to her feet. "I think I'll go back to the cottage and see what's happening."

"It's not two hours yet," Mirabella pointed out. "Not even one hour since we got here."

"I'll just look in," said Antonia feverishly. "Then if there's no news, I—I'll go for a walk."

She refused Michael as an escort. She repulsed Roger's offer of a lift in his car. She was aware of Clare's cool, enquiring regard. And of Mirabella muttering, like a ventriloquist, between unmoving lips: "Let the child go alone, if that's what she wants."

The party broke up.

The woods were melancholy and full of shadows. These last lent to the trees a false distance so that everything was a little out of focus. This strangeness did not affect Antonia. She felt nothing but the relief of getting away from the company of the two young men.

She would, she decided, search the Limes at once. Or, at least, as soon as she had changed her light frock for something less conspicuous. She must hurry too. She would feel easier in mind if she actually saw Mrs. Harker leave the house. Knew its owner to be gone.

She halted suddenly, looking over her shoulder. There was no one to be seen. Nothing to be heard now but the incessant rustling of leaves. Yet she had heard something—or someone—moving on a path parallel to her own.

"Is anyone there?"

Even as she spoke the explanation came to her. Mirabella had sent Michael to shadow her to make certain that she was not taken ill. That she reached the cottage safely. She had frightened herself senselessly, needlessly.

Mentally she shrugged. How lucky that he had not answered. Or shown himself. The last person she wanted to see was Michael. She walked on, hurrying. Not listening any longer for sounds of pursuit. Carefree, she told herself. Even as she did so she was conscious of a feeling of disquiet and, deep within herself, an uneasy vigilance.

She reached the cottage to find it empty but for McKnight.

"I'm not staying," she explained. "I only want to change my frock."

McKnight had just returned from searching her bedroom. He had been hoping to find something that would suggest Antonia's complicity. Her foreknowledge of her friend's disappearance. There had been nothing. He was stuck with his own horrid theory of a sex maniac.

"That will be quite in order, miss," he said heavily.

In her bedroom Antonia pulled open her wardrobe door. There was not much choice. She decided on the black trousers of the tabard suit of the previous evening and a grey sweater meant to be teamed with orange-colored pants.

She hurried down the stairs. Nodded to McKnight and was halfway down the garden path before he had had time to recollect himself. To think of a tactful way of asking where she was going.

At the bottom of the lane she crossed over the road. She walked hurriedly along looking for a weak spot in the garden hedge of the Limes, fearful that she might meet Mrs. Harker. She found one and stood waiting until the road was clear of traffic. Then she pushed her way through, finding herself in an old-fashioned shrubbery. She followed the winding path, picking little bits of twig from her hair and clothes as she walked.

As she drew near the house she heard the sound of a Hoover at work. It was whining its way over what she knew, from more social days, must be the drawing-room floor. It was an odd time to be cleaning, she reflected. But then Mrs. Harker seemed to have turned into an odd sort of woman.

She came to the edge of the gravel sweep. Cautiously she peered out. She could see the side of the house. She also had a view of the front door. To her delight she noticed that one of the drawing-room windows was open at the top. If Mrs. Harker did not close and fasten it before she left, she, Antonia, would have no difficulty in getting in.

The Hoover stopped working. What now? Was Mrs. Harker going upstairs to change her clothes? Or would she merely wash her hands—in the downstair cloakroom perhaps?

The front door opened. Judith Harker came out. She looked neither to the right nor to the left. She walked down the short drive and up the road. Antonia, listening to her footsteps, realised that she had not crossed the road to the stile. She was going towards the main gates of Hone Court. Such formality seemed typical.

Antonia stepped out into the open. The house, she thought, looked very pleasant drowsing in the early evening sunlight. There was nothing in the least sinister. Just to be certain that it was empty she rang the front door bell. She heard it ringing, muted but shrill, far back in the interior. No one answered.

She tried the door. It was locked. She went back to the window she had noticed earlier. She pushed up the lower sash and climbed through. She turned, closing the window behind her.

She found herself, as she had expected, in the drawing room. It was a large, comfortable, and expensive-looking room. It was also very clean. The furniture glowed. The white paint work shone. The silver ornaments were newly polished.

She opened the door into the hall. Here was not only the Hoover but a variety of cleaning utensils, mops, dusters, tins, plastic containers, rubber and housemaid gloves. Such a collection that there came to Antonia a picture, not of the bereft wife sitting alone and laughing to herself. But of the same woman passing the empty days in endless, unaccustomed cleaning.

"Anyone here?" she called. And stood suddenly terrified in case a strange voice answered. There was no sound. The ticking of a clock somewhere close at hand sounded unnaturally loud.

A breath of air rustled the brocade chair frills behind her like the faint swish of a long skirt.

Ignoring the other sitting rooms Antonia went soundlessly up the stairs. She began to feel that the thick smothering carpet everywhere was more a strain to the nerves than any open, honest sound of footsteps.

At the head of the stairs she paused to look about her. She had never been very friendly with the Harkers and so had never been farther than the ground floor.

Closed doors faced her on two sides. At the end of the passage a wall mirror reflected her slight solitary figure.

The silence, the slow drowsy silence of late afternoon, remained unbroken.

Antonia, struggling with a sense of unreality, began to open doors. Each room was empty. Each room was comfortable. As well fitted up as in a first-class hotel—and as impersonal. She came on a particularly handsome two-bedded room with a dressing room opening out of it on one side and a bathroom on the other. It too was unoccupied, although Antonia had an idea that this must have been the Harkers' bedroom when they had been together.

At the end of one of the passages she came on a small bedroom. There were combs and brushes of blond tortoise-shell on the dressing table. A somewhat mannish dark silk dressing gown hung behind the door. The single bed was made up. The room was inhabited—but in a lost, half-hearted way that, to Antonia, did not seem typical of its owner.

She soon satisfied herself that all the rooms on this floor were unoccupied. She found a second back staircase, covered in a plain grey cord carpet, leading to the top floor. At the top of the stairs the carpet ran to right and left.

Antonia's heart was beating fast. Again she stood looking about her. Listening—and hearing only the sound of a bluebottle buzzing its way endlessly across a closed skylight in the roof.

"Dee?" she called and her voice echoed a little, uncertainly. She was frightened now. Her nerves felt tense, strung up. Her

(86)

ears strained to hear, not only any sound from the room about her, but from the floors below. She felt cut off, vulnerable.

She began a hurried search, opening door after door. There was a very modern, up-to-date bathroom. Some of the rooms were empty. Several were pleasantly but plainly furnished. Obviously in happier times this floor would have been occupied by the servants.

Her heart sank as she progressed. It wasn't only that there was no sign of Dee. There was nowhere where she could have been kept. The doors had no keys, only an inner bolt. It would have been perfectly easy to escape on to the roof from any of the windows.

There remained then the cellars. Antonia turned and hurried towards the floor below. She had reached the foot of the back stairs when she halted, her heart seeming to stand still. From downstairs, from the direction of the hall, there had come the sound of movement.

Mrs. Harker had come back.

Swiftly Antonia hurried along the passage. She was not very alarmed. She had only to hear which way Mrs. Harker went and behave accordingly. Towards the kitchen and she, Antonia, would make a soundless dash for the front door. Upstairs and she would slip into one of the disused bedrooms.

She came to the landing and crouched there the better to hear. Mrs. Harker was still moving about in the hall. A door opened, there was a thud—a click. The door closed. Was she putting away the Hoover? Was—?

And then, for no reason that Antonia could understand, terror came flooding over her. Her knees trembled. The palms of her hands were damp. Icy tremors shook her.

The footsteps faded down a passage. A door closed somewhere far away. Now Antonia could hear nothing but her own agitated breathing. See nothing but her own looking-glass image, listening as she listened. Fearful of she knew not what.

In sudden panic she raced down the stairs. She was vaguely surprised to see that the Hoover and the other cleaning articles were in the same place as when she had seen them last. She was just about to cross the hall when again she was brought to a stop.

Someone was fitting a key into the lock of the front door.

Antonia looked about her swiftly. There was a cupboard under the stairs. With someone as tidy and methodical as Mrs. Harker, she reflected, there was certain to be order inside it and a clear space just inside the door.

She opened it. Had time to see that her supposition was correct. Time to see a small stiff brush and a dustpan hanging from two hooks opposite the door. And that an electric floor polisher stood in the corner.

The door was fitted with one of those catches that only needs a pull or push to open or close it. As Antonia pulled the door almost shut she reflected that the Hoover and the other cleaning things must have come from the cupboard. She could only hope that whoever was coming in would not think of replacing them.

She couldn't see the front door but she heard it open and someone enter the hall. She frowned in perplexity. The footsteps sounded lighter than those she had heard before. This, then, was probably Mrs. Harker returning for something. And the other?

The gardener? Yes, that must have been it. He had brought something in. Vegetables perhaps. Or logs. With Mrs. Harker living alone, he was probably more handyman than gardener.

She felt a little ashamed of her previous unreasoning fear.

She put her eye to the crack of the door. A moment later Mrs. Harker's tall angular figure came into view. To Antonia's alarm she paused by the Hoover, one hand resting on it. Very gently Antonia drew the cupboard door together. Tentatively she inched her way farther in. If she could get to the far end she might still remain undiscovered.

She found herself staring at something pale. It was about on a level with her eyes. Its vaguely perceived outline suggested nothing to her. It was neither pleasantly familiar nor terrifyingly strange. It merely represented an obstruction.

She put out an exploring hand. It touched nothing at all. She stretched forward. Her hand met and then closed on something fine, soft, and yet springy. A dusting brush of some sort. A kind of whisk, she told herself. Suddenly her flesh crawled. She was seized with a feeling of utter repugnance, for which she could find no cause. It was as if her brain had delivered an incomplete but fearful message.

Her position now seemed nightmarish. And, as in a nightmare, she must continue on the course she had begun. Reluctantly, trembling a little, her hand went out. She saw it in front of her, the faintest of moving blurs. A blur seeming to have no connection with herself.

And then the seeming dream-like quality vanished. It was succeeded by a sickening sense of reality, of overwhelming horror. Her hand had touched the soft warm cheek of a human face. It traced the eyes, nose, open mouth. Touched again what every shrinking sense now recognised as hair—

She had found Dee.

With a scream of horror, to which her own ears were deaf, she tumbled out of the cupboard. Sat crouched on the tiled floor whilst scream after scream ripped from her throat.

She was aware of Mrs. Harker staring in amazement. Aware of her quick approach. Aware of her harsh voice demanding: "Are you mad?" And: "What are you doing here?" What she was not aware of was her own voice screaming its horrified protest.

Mrs. Harker stooped. Quite deliberately she brought her hand down with a stinging slap on Antonia's cheek. The screaming stopped as if a tap had been turned off. Antonia just crouched there, white faced except for the mark of the other woman's hand.

"And now perhaps," said Mrs. Harker grimly, "you'll have the goodness to tell me what is the matter with you?"

As she spoke there came a new sound. That of the drawing-room window being pushed up. A moment later Michael Chant came hurrying through the drawing-room door into the hall.

"Antonia! What is it?" He dropped on one knee beside the girl. "Don't look like that. You're safe now."

"As far as I know Miss Hughes was always safe," said Judith harshly.

Antonia clutched Michael's arm, forgetting her earlier suspicion of him. "In the cupboard," she croaked. "Dee—she's in there."

"What?" Judith changed colour. She started forward. She peered into the cupboard. "Good God!" she muttered blankly. And to Michael: "You'd better get her out."

"The torch—in my pocket," Antonia muttered. She felt curiously empty, drained of all feeling. She also had the illusion that she was about to leave the ground and float.

She heard Judith's voice, as sharp and swift as the slap she had administered. "Pull yourself together, girl," it ordered. "This is no time to go off in a genteel faint."

Michael came out from the cupboard. His face was white but he spoke steadily enough, as he straightened up. "Buck up, Antonia," he said. "It's not Dee in there. It's Beatrice—Beatrice Lynham."

"Not Dee—?" Antonia scrambled unsteadily to her feet. She was aware of a feeling of incredulity. It was followed by an overwhelming sensation of relief.

Michael was speaking to Judith. "We can't move her. It's a matter for the police."

"Let me look." Judith took the torch. She bent and peered into the cupboard. "Yes, I see what you mean," she said slowly. "Better ring Hobday—and your aunt too. Make my apologies to her. You'll find a telephone in the drawing room." She turned to Antonia. "And now perhaps you'll tell me what you and Michael were doing in my house?"

"I don't know what Michael was doing." Suspicion was coming back into Antonia's mind. "I was looking for Dee."

Judith stared. She laughed shortly. "Sounds reasonable," she admitted.

When Michael returned he said, "Hobday is coming as soon as he has telephoned the police in Winstead. So we should soon have everyone here."

"That," said Judith dryly, "is indeed good news." She rose to her feet. "I think we should all have a drink to steady our nerves. One way or another the next hour is going to be a bit of a strain for all of us."

She led the way back into the drawing room. A handsome mahogany piece of furniture turned out to be a cocktail cabinet. She busied herself with bottles and glasses.

Michael began to explain his appearance in the house. She cut him short. "Leave it," she said curtly. "You can explain yourself to the police. I'm past caring."

She carried a glass to where Antonia stood, ghastly pale and hesitating on the threshold of the room. "Drink this. A shot of Vodka. It's only a drop but it'll pull you together."

When she saw how Antonia's hand shook she took the glass and put it to the girl's lips. She tipped the contents into her mouth. "That's better. Now sit down somewhere. All the chairs are comfortable." She picked up her own glass. "Michael, you help yourself. There are cigarettes too, if anyone wants one."

Silence fell on the room. An unreal silence it seemed to Antonia. Unreal too that she should have broken into Mrs. Harker's house. Unreal that Beatrice Lynham should lie dead in a cupboard under the stairs—or, indeed, anywhere else. And still more unreal that she, Antonia, should be sitting in Mrs. Harker's drawing room with that lady sitting comfortably opposite, her long legs stretched out in front of her, glass in hand, weather-beaten face wearing no particular expression. Certainly not the furious and malicious one to which Antonia had grown accustomed.

Soon they heard the sound of an approaching car.

"See who it is, Michael," said Judith. "It seems too early for the police." She stayed where she was, idly swishing the whisky about in her glass, idly staring down at it. What thoughts passed behind her expressionless face the girl could not even guess.

Michael returned, followed by Septimus Finch. "I'm sorry to break in on you like this," said the latter, "particularly since I seem to be the first to arrive. Hobday gave me a message from Superintendent Bollard, asking me to meet him here, not, I imagine, officially." He passed her his warrant card: "But because by a series of coincidences, I found myself mixed up in this matter of Miss Sumner's disappearance."

"Detective Chief Inspector Septimus Finch," read Mrs. Harker aloud. "You are very welcome—and I mean that. I seem to find myself in what is usually described as an invidious situation."

She smiled at him, liking what she saw. She was not deceived by the newcomer's lazy easygoing gait. She knew an athletic body when she saw one. To her his soft voice was an affectation and not one to which she objected. His air of mild somnolence, she saw, was due to no more than the absurdly long lashes which did so much to hide his eyes.

For his part Finch recognised in Mrs. Harker a man's woman. Still attractive in a back-slapping, hard-drinking fashion. Although the attraction was not, he reflected, one that was likely to occur to the young Antonia.

"So you are a police officer," Michael commented. "We thought you must be one."

"But that is just a coincidence, isn't it? You didn't come to Hone because of Dee?" Antonia looked very small and rather lost in the large room, but she asked the question steadily enough, despite the horror still shadowing her face.

Finch shook his head. "I had a week's leave due to me and came down to play golf with Inspector Engleman who is an old friend. I was not expecting to be involved in anything mysterious or untoward." He looked at Mrs. Harker and added enquiringly: "If either word fits the case?"

Judith gave a harsh laugh. "Mysterious? Yes. Untoward is not nearly strong enough. Miss Hughes here came to look for her friend, whom she thought I might have locked up somewhere in the house. She didn't find her. She did find another girl, Beatrice Lynham, dead in the cupboard under the stairs. She had been strangled."

Finch was startled. "Beatrice Lynham?"

Judith smiled thinly. "*You* sound surprised. How do you think I feel?"

Finch thought of the imminent arrival of the Winstead Superintendent. "D'you mind if I have a look?"

"Help yourself. Michael has a torch."

Finch looked at him. "I think you can hold it steady."

"I've already seen her," Michael answered briefly. They left the room.

Antonia shivered. "I didn't know that. I mean that Beatrice had been strangled. It was—dark in the cupboard."

Judith nodded. "And you didn't wait." She added: "Had you seen her today?"

"No." Antonia's expression changed. She had remembered that she had not seen Sebastian either—except hanging about in front of his house as if waiting for someone.

Judith looked at her cynically. "No need to tell the police anything they don't ask about."

Finch and Michael returned. Michael looked pale but composed. The detective was his usual bland self.

"Curious thing," he murmured in his soft voice. "Obviously the girl hasn't been there long."

Antonia began to tremble again. "I think I heard someone put her there. At least, I heard someone moving about in the hall—and then walking towards the back of the house. I even heard a door close. The back door I suppose it was."

"Did you see anything?" Finch asked.

Antonia shook her head. "I was on the first-floor landing and afraid of being seen myself. The hall is so light. At the time I took it for granted that it was Mrs. Harker come back for something she had forgotten. Later I decided that it must have been the gardener I had heard."

"He isn't here today." Judith turned from the cocktail cabinet, glass in hand. "A drink for you, Mr. Finch? Michael?"

They refused.

"What made you come back to the house, Mrs. Harker?"

"I was going to spend the evening with Mrs. Chant. I had almost reached the gates of Hone Court when I remembered that I had left the back door unlocked." She glanced at Antonia. "A window, too, it seems."

Finch smiled. "You certainly made it easy for an intruder. And yet even with doors locked and windows closed, houses aren't burglarproof—even to amateurs." He stopped speaking as the front door bell rang. "This, I fancy, is where I retire."

Mrs. Harker smiled grimly. "Don't be too certain of that. Superintendent Bollard is not going to like this a bit." She tipped up her glass and drained it at one go.

A moment later Michael showed Hobday into the room. The Hone constable looked very solemn. His eyes were anxious, since the situation was, he felt, beyond him. "Afternoon, ma'am," he said to Mrs. Harker. He eased his collar with one finger. "Though to be sure good evening would be nearer the mark."

"We're none of us in the mood to cavil if you had greeted us with Heil Hitler," said Mrs. Harker tartly. "What's the drill now?"

"Well, ma'am," said Hobday doubtfully, "I reckon I should view the body." He ventured it cautiously and with an anxious glance in Finch's direction.

Finch waved a muscular but well-kept hand. "You go ahead and look. Take Mr. Chant with you. He has a torch. I shall sit here and wait for Superintendent Bollard."

"Thank you, sir." Hobday had been speculating rather unhappily on his way to the Limes as to what the Yard man might be up to. To find him doing no more than lounging lazily in one of the big armchairs in the drawing room was a great relief. He left the room with Michael.

The three people left behind fell silent. Each was following in thought the two who had gone. After a moment they heard Hobday give a startled exclamation.

"The poor maid," he said. When he returned to the drawing room most of his ruddy colour had gone. So had much of his former nervousness.

"I don't rightly feel qualified to ask any questions," he said, "but I must request you all to wait in the room until the Superintendent gets here. And, hoping you'll take no offence, I shall sit with you until he arrives."

"And if we do take offence?" Mrs. Harker demanded.

Hobday looked at her. "I shall sit here just the same, ma'am," he said apologetically but firmly.

SEVEN

Superintendent Bollard was a crafty but somewhat slow-thinking man. At the moment he was a gloomy man. He did not like murder cases, particularly when better-class people were involved. It was apt to lead to awkwardnesses—and awkwardness, as far as it affected his career, was something he liked to avoid.

When he came into the drawing room he greeted Mrs. Harker with a nice mixture of melancholy and respect. He saw Finch and a thin satisfied smile parted his lips. As the Yard man had suspected, the Superintendent did not see why he should not take advantage of the other's undoubted experience without giving him any of the credit.

In answer to Bollard's request for a room in which he could interview witnesses, Mrs. Harker suggested the dining room. There he retired, taking Finch with him and collecting Engleman from the hall on his way.

"This is the very deuce," he complained as soon as the door was shut. "The Harkers are well known. Very generous to local charities—and that includes the police orphanage. And I—well, I've always admired her. A fine-looking woman. A fine figure on a horse. Very pleasant to meet too." He looked at Finch, hoping he had taken the point. After a significant pause he added: "Not the sort to descend to violence, I'm sure you'll agree."

The three men discussed the disappearance of Dee Sumner for a few minutes—but without overtones and with little anxiety. Bollard, Finch reflected, seemed blissfully unaware of the hurricane of publicity that would follow if Dee Sumner was found to have been murdered. Safer for him to arrest a dozen local bigwigs than to fail to find *her* killer.

The Superintendent produced a notebook. "This other girl —Beatrice Lynham? Did you meet her?"

"Yes." Finch did not elaborate. "Mrs. Chant described her as a nasty prying girl. If that does describe her it may account for what has happened to her. On the other hand Mrs. Chant may be prejudiced. Miss Lynham was Sebastian Chant's current girl friend."

"D'you think he—?" Bollard made a graphic gesture towards his own throat.

"He's strong enough to have carried her without trouble and he knows the house. On the other hand, why suddenly become violent? To do that he must have had a very strong motive. A motive not apparent at the moment."

Bollard grunted. He sent for a constable who knew shorthand, and for Antonia. She entered with a kind of forlorn dignity. She looked very small as she sat facing the three tall men across the table. At a hint from Finch, the Superintendent drew from her an account of what had been said or done on the previous evening at Hone Court. She went on to speak of George Harker's warning and of her own decision to make certain that her friend was not shut up somewhere in the Limes. She agreed with Bollard that what she had done was illegal.

She gave a straightforward account of her search of the house. From it two points of interest emerged. The first, that Antonia's reason for thinking that it was Mrs. Harker whom she had heard in the hall, had been because of the intruder's unhurried movements, which had suggested not only a familiarity with the house but a right to be there.

The second was that Beatrice's cheek had been soft and

faintly warm to the touch, suggesting that the girl had been dead only a short time.

"When you were in the woods on your way here, did you see or hear anyone else?" Bollard asked.

"I thought I heard someone else in the woods."

"Yes?"

Antonia said in a low voice, "That was all. I just thought. I might have been wrong."

"On the other hand you might have been right?"

Antonia shivered. She paled still further. "Yes."

When she had left the room Bollard remarked: "Something wrong there. That young lady was composed enough until I mentioned the woods."

"Probably she's come round to suspecting that it was Michael Chant she heard," Engleman suggested. "And that he wasn't following her as much as hurrying past her on his way to meet Beatrice Lynham. It would make her take a rather different view of that young man."

Finch nodded his agreement. "Tall, dark, and gruesome."

Michael Chant's story was brief. His reason for following Miss Hughes had been that she had looked ill. His aunt had been afraid that she might collapse before reaching the cottage. He had not expected that she would be allowed by the police to stay there so he had circled the cottage and waited for her to re-emerge, concealing himself behind the garage, hoping to join her in her walk. She had reappeared with such an air of purpose that he had realised that she was up to something. He had, therefore, followed her at a discreet distance.

He had taken up a position on higher ground in the shrubbery of the Limes. He had seen Mrs. Harker leave the house. Seen Antonia enter it and Mrs. Harker re-enter. This last had left him wondering what to do for the best. He had just decided to ring the front door bell and distract Mrs. Harker in conversation when he had heard Antonia screaming.

He declared that he had not seen anyone else about. Nor had he heard anyone enter or leave by the back door. From where he had been standing close to the hedge, anything but a

(97)

loud sound would have been drowned by that of passing cars, for at that time of day the road was busy.

He declared that he had no idea why anyone should have wanted to kill Beatrice Lynham. He agreed with Antonia's recollection of what Beatrice had said about the mist. He himself did not attach much importance to it since Beatrice had been a contrary sort of girl. She often disagreed with what was said just to annoy. Her boy friend, he averred, had been Keith Vesey.

"Innocent as a new-born babe. The young man I mean," Bollard grunted after Michael had left. "The truth is that he could have strangled the girl and put her body in the cupboard. And then judged it expedient to see what was going on, and so returned."

"Yet planting the body in this house was a stupid thing to do," Engleman remarked. "It shows the murderer was someone who knew of Mrs. Harker's feelings about Miss Sumner and also that she was already suspect."

"It wouldn't have seemed stupid if Miss Hughes hadn't heard it being done," Finch pointed out. "But for that, when the body was found, it would have been thought that Mrs. Harker, having killed the girl, had dumped her body in the cupboard, meaning to move it again when some more suitable place had been prepared."

Said Bollard heavily: "But it is possible that Mrs. Harker did, in fact, strangle the girl."

"It was Byron who said 'Revenge is sweet'—particularly to a woman," Finch rejoined amiably.

Bollard forced a smile. "I'd prefer to know what *you* thought." He hoped that he was not going to dislike the Yard man.

"I think that Judith Harker is the obvious suspect—and yet if she left the house with the intention of fetching the body, where was it? The other side of the main road? In that case it seems unlikely that she would have moved it when the road was at its busiest."

Bollard nodded. A sound man, this Finch, after all. "Better have Mrs. Harker in—"

Before he could finish his sentence there was a loud knock

on the door. It flew open. A big, bald, boisterous man burst in. This was the police surgeon, Dr. Haynes.

"Evening, gentlemen," he cried. And then: "I thought you might like an interim report. Deceased has been dead not longer than two hours—probably less. She was hoist with her own petard. Or, rather, strangled with her own necklace. It got broken during the melee. I imagine that, before that happened something hung from it—a charm, locket. Something of that sort."

"It was an old-fashioned gold locket," said Finch. "I saw it earlier today."

Dr. Haynes nodded. "Find that and you'll find the place where the murder took place but not, I fancy, the motive. There are no signs of her having been sexually assaulted, so that's out."

Bollard regarded him gloomily. "And the murderer? Any signs as to his identity?"

"Let me see." Dr. Haynes stroked his chin. Finch fancied the two men must often have annoyed each other with a display such as this. "The murderer was active, determined, and strong. Not abnormally strong, mark you. Just strong. The girl put up no fight. She may have given a cry. It would have been the only one. She must have been taken by surprise, thrown to the ground and strangled. Easy enough. The murder weapon was already conveniently round her neck." He hesitated, looked almost slyly at Bollard, then remarked: "None of my business, of course. But that gold chain was a good one. Must have cost quite a bit. May have been a present from the murderer. From her clothes I wouldn't have thought that she could have afforded to buy it herself." He wagged his head. "Nasty cheap material. Shoddy work. I ought to know. My father was a tailor."

Dr. Haynes distributed a wide and cheerful smile. Remarked: "Tell you more when I've had a rummage," and bounded from the room.

Bollard sighed heavily. "A good chap, Dr. Haynes. Reliable. Enthusiastic. He keeps all sorts of bits and pieces in bottles. A sort of private Black Museum." Adding in a brooding voice:

"If only the silly b—— wouldn't sound like the stooge in a music hall act."

Judith Harker was the last witness. She came in seeming relaxed, handsome, and self-possessed. The staring, ravaged look had gone from her face, the tautness from her body. Finch looked at her with renewed interest. He realised just what an enormous effort of will this must entail.

She sat down at the table. "This is a terrible thing to have happened. That unfortunate girl."

"You knew her?"

"I had met her. A poor little dab of a creature. Mr. Chant was attracted to her, so she was somewhat more in evidence than one would have expected."

"And you can give no explanation of how she came to be here—under the stairs?"

Judith Harker frowned thoughtfully. Absently she picked a bit of tobacco off her lower lip. "I can't help feeling that someone put her there because, in some minds, I am already connected with the disappearance of Miss Sumner."

"You know about that?"

"It was the reason for Miss Hughes's extraordinary behaviour —so she tells me."

"You wish to charge her with breaking into your house?"

"Heavens, no! I rather admire her for it." Judith took a slim platinum cigarette case from her pocket and lit another cigarette. "Will any of you?" She held out the case. "I suppose it was natural for Miss Hughes to suspect that her friend might be here."

"And she is not?" Bollard asked heavily.

Judith shrugged. She blew the smoke frim her cigarette down her nose. "How should I know? If you search the house—and you should certainly do so—you may find Miss Sumner's body, just as that of Miss Lynham has been found."

Bollard was shocked, uncomfortable. "Mrs. Harker—" he began and broke off.

Judith Harker smiled at him, seemingly quite at her ease. "Superintendent—" she mocked.

"We should, of course, like to find Miss Sumner," said Bollard in a tone of rebuke, "but not here. And not under these circumstances." He turned to Finch. "Are there any questions you would like to put?"

"I should like to know what Mrs. Harker had intended to do to Miss Sumner?"

Judith's fine eyes met his steadily enough. "I meant to lay her face open with my riding crop," she said simply.

Bollard's expression of outrage was almost ludicrous. "Mrs. Harker, think what you are saying," he besought her in scandalized tones.

"Superintendent, I am thinking. And what I intended is so much less than what I now suspect may have happened."

"But what you intended is illegal."

"And it is not illegal to take away one's husband because one is younger and more beautiful? I know. That was why I intended to adjust the balance."

"And that is all you intended?" Bollard sounded relieved. He did not realise, as Finch had done, that such treatment could sear and pucker a lovely face forever.

"It would have been enough," said Judith truthfully.

"Why not have attacked her in London?" Finch asked.

"There were too many people about. And at night, when there weren't too many people about"—Judith's lips curled—"Miss Sumner always had a male escort."

Finch looked at Judith curiously. "Miss Sumner is a big strong girl."

"She is a big girl," Judith corrected, "and I suppose reasonably fit. I am the strong one."

Again Bollard looked uncomfortable. "Mrs. Harker, I believe you left London last Thursday in pursuit of Miss Sumner?"

"That is so. But two miles this side of Maidstone I found I had a flat tyre. By the time I had changed it there seemed no point in taking up the chase again."

"So you stopped and had a meal somewhere?" Bollard encouraged her.

A faint flicker of amusement passed over the hard face. "I had a picnic basket in the car. I drove a little way into some woods and had a meal there. A cold game pie, a salad, half a bottle of a rather nice hock and some grapes."

"And you didn't stop anywhere else on the road?"

"I did not."

"But later you did try and satisfy yourself that Miss Sumner was at her cottage?" Finch asked.

Judith looked at him. "I satisfied myself that she was there—or so I thought."

"How was that?" Finch's voice was very soft and drawling. Bollard and Engleman had grown suddenly still, expectant.

"I walked down to the Thatched Cottage twice. The first time about eight o'clock. The mist, which had been a bit thick, was thinning out then. I was a little surprised to see the cottage looking so shut up. No windows open. No lights showing. Yes," she added reflectively, "even then that struck me for a moment as odd. I suppose because I had been so certain in my own mind that she *would* be there."

"You didn't go right up to the cottage?"

"No, I had no intention of calling on her that evening." The steely note was back in Mrs. Harker's voice. "In fact, I didn't want to be seen and perhaps scare her off. I kept in the field opposite, hidden by the hedge."

Finch recalled the position of the garage and that of the gate into the field. "You didn't look into the garage?"

Judith shook her head. "The light was failing. The windows are too high up for one to glance in automatically as one passes. Besides, I took it for granted the car was there and Miss Sumner probably at Hone Court."

"And you went down later to have another look at the cottage?" Bollard prompted.

Judith was silent a moment. Then she said: "It was after eleven when I paid my second visit. By then some cows had been put in the field. They were lying under the big chestnut tree. I heard them chewing the cud. I smelt them too. I even fell over one. I got up and moved away. Then it stood staring at me. Poor creature, it didn't expect some foolish human being to come sprawling over it."

There was, Finch saw, some point approaching that Judith Harker did not want to recall, far less mention.

Bollard prodded her towards it. "The cottage?" he cried impatiently. "What about the cottage?"

Judith drew on her cigarette. "This time—" she said, staring down at the polished top of the table, "this time the mist had cleared. I saw a light at an upstair window. It streamed out through a small gap in the drawn curtains."

"What did you do?"

"I went back to the gate leading from the field and down the lane to the cottage," said Judith in a flat, unemotional voice. "I walked all round it, keeping on the grass. I thought I'd look in through the windows but the curtains were drawn everywhere with not a chink showing." She paused, then added: "I could hear the telephone inside the cottage ringing and ringing. As I turned to go home it stopped ringing. And the light upstairs went off."

Bollard was frowning. "The telephone ringing and no one answering it. Didn't you think that strange?"

Mrs. Harker studied the bright end of her cigarette. "Now it does seem strange. At the time," she spoke with intense bitterness, "at the time I thought that Miss Sumner was in bed with some man and did not want to be interrupted."

To the three men it was clear that Judith Harker thought that the man had been her husband. It was clear too that there was an alternative. This was that she was a liar—and a superb actress, giving a superb performance.

The three people in the drawing room had long fallen silent. Judith Harker was drinking steadily without its having any obvious effect. Antonia felt sick. She had no heart for conversation. She sat trying not to hear the sounds from the hall. Or, if she must hear them, not to speculate as to what they portended. Michael had made several tentative attempts to rouse one or other of his two companions. Now he too pursued his own thoughts.

The door opened. Septimus Finch came in.

"Turn the lights on, will you?" Judith said. "We've all been too sunk in gloom to bother." She rose to her feet as he did so. She smiled at him, blinking a little in the sudden illumination. "I imagine that nothing else has been found hidden in my house?"

"Nothing."

"Then what happens next?"

"The Winstead police will be here for some time still. I am hoping that I can give Miss Hughes a lift back to her cottage."

Michael stirred. "When I rang up my aunt she gave me strict instructions to take you to Hone Court to sleep," he told Antonia.

The girl shrank a little. "I shall be quite all right at the cottage, thank you."

"Better spend the night at Hone Court," Finch advised. "I'll drive you there. We can call at the cottage first for anything you need."

Michael looked amused but puzzled. "Can't you drive me too?"

Finch shook his head. "Sorry, but I want to talk to Miss Hughes," he said blandly.

"Is that strictly ethical?" Judith demanded.

"Miss Hughes can always refuse."

"Why should I?" said Antonia wearily.

"It was only an idea," said Judith. "At a time like this one finds one's head filled with ideas—mostly evasive ones."

Finch turned to Antonia. "Shall we go?"

"That's right. You two go," said Judith. "Michael shall keep me company." She looked at him. "As for Beatrice Lynham, I will promise not to suspect you of killing her, if you will promise not to suspect me."

Michael said nothing. Only when Finch and Antonia had left the house he remarked: "What was all that about? I had an impression that I was getting a decided brush off—from both the Chief Inspector and Antonia."

Judith was pouring herself another drink. "Help yourself," she invited with a wave of her hand. And then, sinking back into her chair: "Hasn't it occurred to you that you might be suspected of killing that girl and putting her in the cupboard? You knew Dee Sumner too. If you had seen her you would have recognised her." She added maliciously: "I don't know what the police think but obviously those are ideas that have already occurred to little Miss Hughes." She looked at Michael and laughed. "So, under those rather old-fashioned nice manners of yours, you do have a bad temper? I've sometimes wondered."

Outside the last of the daylight was fading. The road lay plain before Finch's car but in the lane between high hedges the evening had become almost night. The outline of the Thatched Cottage had dissolved, one with the dark woods. A single lighted window seemed to hang incongruously, existing in a void.

Finch stopped the car. He turned to look at his passenger. His heart smote him. She was naturally a small girl. Now she appeared to have shrunk. Her face too looked small, pale, and pinched.

"It does not seem reasonable to suppose," she said in a small precise voice, "that we can have two unconnected mysteries. Since Beatrice Lynham is dead it seems to me that Dee must be dead too."

"That," said Finch gently, "seems a fair assessment of the position." He added, "I hope you won't add to your unhappiness by suspecting anyone in particular. The police aren't doing so. Believe me, there is not enough evidence."

Antonia smiled, a small stiff smile. "The police can afford to be impartial. I could not bear to find later on that I had been friendly with—the person who had killed Dee."

The second search of the cottage was over. Finch spoke to the constable on duty. He was aware, as he did so, of Antonia's quick footsteps overhead on the polished boards. Of drawers hurriedly pulled out. Of the wardrobe door opening and closing. They were all sounds of panic flight barely contained.

The police constable told him that they had found further proof that Miss Sumner had been in the cottage. A long golden hair on the settee. Some face powder spilt on the carpet in front of her dressing table.

There had been no obvious sign of the presence of anyone

else in the cottage. An examination by the forensic laboratory of the dust collected might yield more positive results.

The extended search had resulted in the finding of a number of cigarette ends close to the hedge in the field opposite. They were of the same brand as those smoked by Judith Harker. The ground had proved too hard to have taken any footprints.

Antonia came flying down the stairs. "I'm ready," she said breathlessly. "Do let us go." She looked haunted, wild eyed. As if, at any moment, she might break down and scream.

The Chants' wing of Hone Court was brightly lit upstairs and down. A light shone above the side door. Almost before the car drew up the door itself flew open. Mirabella hastened out.

"So you have brought her, Chief Inspector. Antonia, my sweet child!" Her voice sharpened a little. "But where is Michael?"

"He stayed with Mrs. Harker," said Antonia wearily.

"W-ell, I suppose now she has no one else," said Mirabella but she said it grudgingly. "Come in, Chief Inspector." She clasped her plump hands. Altered her tone of voice. "*Please come in*. Have some supper. Or, at least, a drink. It's so terrible knowing nothing."

"A drink would be very nice. I haven't much time. I have to meet Inspector Engleman." Finch followed his hostess into the house.

Clare Vesey was coming down the stairs. She was wearing grey slacks and a pale yellow sweater. Finch recognised in her the desperate-looking young woman whom he had seen with Roger Frampton that morning. She was, he supposed, good-looking. Unusual anyway, with her pale colouring and fine-boned lankiness.

She paused on the stairs, looking down at him from her superior position. A strange look, neither hostile nor friendly. It was more one of recognition, he thought. Recognition on a purely impersonal level.

"There you are, Clare," said Mirabella. "Take Antonia into the kitchen and see she eats something. Come in here, Chief— Oh, I shall go on calling you Mr. Finch. The other is too much of a mouthful. I haven't the patience—" She broke off. "There, I'm an absurd old woman but I am too old for all these goings on. Dee disappearing. Poor Beatrice dead."

Finch looked at her with inward amusement. So, from now on it was to be poor Beatrice. A wise decision perhaps. She had her nephew and her husband to consider. She herself was not above suspicion.

When they both had drinks and were comfortably installed in two chairs proportionate to their size, Mirabella remarked, "I suppose there must be a connection between these two terrible happenings. Although what it is I cannot imagine since Beatrice and Dee had never met."

"Are you certain of that?"

"As certain as one can be. Dee was, in her way, a celebrity. Beatrice would certainly have claimed acquaintanceship with her if she could. As it was when Dee was spoken of she grew a little sulky, resentful. No, I feel certain they had never met." Mirabella looked at Finch. "When Michael telephoned he said that Beatrice's body had been found in a cupboard at the Limes?"

"Yes, by Miss Hughes." Finch told her the facts. Mirabella listened, pursing and unpursing her lips. Her expression was anxious and she seemed uneasy.

The door opened. Clare came in and Mirabella introduced Finch to her.

"Antonia is going to share my room," she told her hostess. "There's a second bed."

Mirabella stared. "What an excellent idea. And all your own I dare say." She muttered something Finch could not catch. If Michael had been there he would have recognised the word "imperatorial" on her lips.

Finch took his leave. He got into his car. He was just about to start the engine when Sebastian appeared round the side of the house with every appearance of furtive haste.

"I've been hanging about looking out for you ever since I got home and heard that Beatrice had been murdered. Wanted to speak to you before that chap Bollard arrests me."

"Be my guest," Finch invited, with a wave of his hand towards the seat beside him. He let in the clutch. "It would be as well to get away from the house." He drove round the bend of the drive and stopped the car.

"Tell me," he said in his murmuring voice, "what makes you think Bollard will arrest you?"

"You tell me how Beatrice was killed."

"She was throttled by the gold chain she wore round her neck."

Sebastian groaned. "That settles it. I gave her that chain. She saw it in a jeweller's window in Hone. Set her heart on it. So I gave it to her."

Said Finch dryly: "I imagine that few gifts are given with the idea of using them as lethal weapons on the recipient at a later date."

Sebastian gave a deep sigh. "That poor kid. Yet all I can do is think of the ghastly position it has left me in."

"What makes you think it so ghastly?"

Sebastian's innocent-seeming gaze came back to Finch, peering at him through the near darkness. "Wouldn't you, if you were in my shoes?" He shook his head, adding gloomily: "But you wouldn't be in my shoes. I wouldn't be either if I'd had the slightest sense. All those girls—" He fell silent, leaning a little forward, podgy hands clasped. Eyes staring straight in front of him as if looking down a long, long road peopled with innumerable damsels. After a few moments uneasy contemplation he declared, "But I've finished with all that from now on. A reformed character. Not that that will be any virtue on my part. Don't suppose any girl will trust herself in my company after this."

"I think that's going a bit far. You're not the only suspect. Not even a particularly likely one."

Sebastian gave him a rather helpless look. "But I shall be when it's known that I was in the woods this afternoon—just about the time Beatrice must have been killed."

"Were you seen?"

"Of course I was seen," was the testy reply. "Why d'you think I'm telling you all this?"

Finch was amused. "You really are a remarkable man."

Sebastian looked delighted. "Am I?" His pleasure faded. "I'm an old fool. Otherwise I wouldn't be in this mess."

"Well, suppose you begin at the beginning—wherever you think that to be."

"I imagine," said Sebastian doubtfully, "that it would be when I found Mirabella wasn't anywhere about and I went and had lunch with the dancers. Beatrice was there. Sitting on the opposite side of the table farther down. She seemed in excellent spirits, laughing and fooling around with the young fellow sitting next to her. I don't mind telling you I was a bit narked. After the meal I waylaid her. Suggested we should go out together but she said she wanted to wash her hair. I suggested the evening but she wouldn't do that either. Seemed not exactly offended but as if she wanted to break with me altogether. And that was odd because, up to then, she'd made most of the running."

"Perhaps she had hoped for a more permanent arrangement."

"She did suggest it once or twice." Sebastian looked at Finch uneasily. "And once or twice it did enter my mind that she thought I might get Mirabella to divorce me and marry her instead. Sounds daft, doesn't it? Daresay there was no truth in the suspicion."

"Suppose we go back to this afternoon."

"Right oh! I had meant to tell you anyway." Sebastian paused, gathering his wandering thoughts. "Where was I? Oh, yes! I'd just said that Beatrice seemed to have gone right off me. So I went to my study and did some work on the accounts. I usually do begin on them about this time of the year. I saw the gang off to Winstead"—Finch thought it typical of the little man that he should think of them as "the gang." "Then my wife turned up with some story of Dee having disappeared." He added gloomily, "If only I'd paid some attention to what she was saying I shouldn't have got myself into this mess."

"You mean you wouldn't have gone off to the woods?"

"I'd have been listening to Mirabella instead, wouldn't I? But there it was. I went back to the accounts. To sulk really. Then I found I'd run out of cigarettes. So I decided to walk into Hone and get some." (One of the advantages of village life is that, if the shops are shut, you just knock on the back door and get what you want.) "I was walking along the footpath on the far side of the main road—"

"Let's get this straight. You'd crossed the field and gone down the lane?" Finch was thinking that, if that were so, Sebastian might have been seen by McKnight. It would be some sort of corroboration of his story.

Sebastian shook his head. "That particular path through the wood branches. One path goes across the field. The other runs to the main road and a stile. There's another stile opposite and a path leading to the village. Well, I was hurrying along this far path when I saw Beatrice in front of me, walking slowly along—"

"What time was this?"

Sebastian looked at him. "Do wish you wouldn't keep trying to pin a chap down. Because, quite frankly, old boy—Chief Inspector—I'm not a great one for worrying about time. Take breakfast now. I just sit on at the table reading the *Times*. When I see the dancers come out on to the lawn I go and join them. And so it goes on." Sebastian considered. "Tell you what, you ask my wife what time she got back here. I must have set off for the village about an hour later—give or take fifteen minutes," after which solution of the problem he looked at Finch with some satisfaction.

Finch nodded. "So you saw Miss Lynham?"

"Yes and I called out to her. She turned round and saw me. Spoke to me sour as a quince. Told me to go away and leave her alone. At that I got angry too. Said, if that was the way she wanted it, it was all right by me. And I walked on. Looked back once. She was standing just where I'd left her. When she saw me turn she made a gesture for me to keep on walking, so I did. I felt pretty sore, I can tell you. There didn't seem to be anyone about. It was quiet in the woods." He feel silent a moment. Then again he looked closely at Finch. "That's how I came to hear her. Because of the quiet I mean. I'd nearly reached the village by then."

"But what did you hear?"

Sebastian looked at him. "She screamed," he said simply.

EIGHT

Finch was startled at Sebastian's remark. "You heard Miss Lynham scream?" He was recalling what the police surgeon had said. "She may have given a cry. It would have been the only one!"

Sebastian nodded. "It was faint and far away but that's what it was. A scream—short and cut off. I turned and started to run back. I came to where I had seen her last. She wasn't there. No one was there. I called and listened but there wasn't a sound. It was all damned queer. I began to search for her. A young couple—visitors—at least I didn't know them—came along and stopped to stare. So I stopped searching and stared back until they went away. Later on some school kids came from the direction of the village. I gave them a handful of coppers and told them to hop it."

It had grown dark while Sebastian had been speaking. Now he was no more than a small hunched figure of a man, with a pale blur of a face and two uneasily moving blurs which were his hands.

He cleared his throat. "Nothing queer about my giving them money. I like kids and they know it. Sometimes, before an outing of some sort, I'll meet them everywhere. Never the same lot twice. They know I'd spot that. A sort of conspiracy to get a bit of extra spending money. But I don't mind."

"You told them to go away?"

"Yes—you see by then I'd decided that that's what I was going to do myself. That Beatrice and the chap she'd been waiting for were somewhere there, lying in the bracken. So I shoo-ed off the kids and walked back into Hone and got my cigarettes. Where? At Scanlons, a corner shop. A decent old couple. I've known them all my life. They were just making tea so I stayed and had a cup and a bit of a natter. Then, since I was still feeling a bit put out, I decided to go and see one of my tenants. Fellow who wants a new roof. So I walked over the downs almost to the next village. A goodish walk but then I'm the biggest landowner in this part of Kent. It was beginning to get dark when I got home—"

"Was that why you didn't notice a policeman standing outside the Limes and the cars in front of the house?"

"Didn't pass the Limes. Old Logan—chap who wanted a new roof—was driving into Winstead, so he ran me home first."

"Did you see anyone you knew while on the way to Mr. Logan's?"

"Saw Roger Frampton. He was sitting alone outside his cottage. Struck me he must be lonely but I didn't feel like talking. Just waved and went on."

Finch thought that Sebastian's story had the ring of truth. The course of events he described sounded typical of the owner of Hone Court. He said aloud: "I feel certain the police will need a great deal more evidence before they arrest you. They may be a bit peeved that you didn't get in touch with them straightaway. But, at least, you have told me and I can tell Inspector Engleman. So don't worry too much. And a word of advice. Don't go off anywhere on your own. Then, if something more should happen you will have that most valuable asset, an alibi."

Sebastian was grateful. "Shan't stay with Mirabella," he declared darkly. "Give her any encouragement and she'll try and prove I was with the Archbishop of Canterbury at the relevant time." He climbed out of the car. "Clergymen tend to be thick on the ground on her side of the family. A damned dreary lot. Low Church to a man." Adding hastily: "Not that that's anything against them. Come to be like them myself I shouldn't be surprised. No dancing, no girls. Only the straight and narrow."

He nodded a farewell and walked away, rather dejectedly, Finch thought, towards the house.

Clare and Antonia were in the room they had agreed to share. It was a large comfortable room. It had twin beds, a wardrobe like the side of a house and a view over the front lawns to the woods beyond.

Downstairs time had dragged. Michael had not come back from the Limes. Mirabella had insisted on a musical evening. Sebastian had been morose, starting at every sound. Finally his wife's choice of records had driven him from the room. By ten o'clock the two girls had been glad to say good night and go upstairs to bed.

Clare had pushed the window up. She was leaning out, her arms resting on the windowsill. The moon had risen above the downs. The garden lay spread below her with great clarity. A few statues glimmered palely against the dark background of the woods. All was dreamlike, beautiful and unreal.

"The peace of it," Clare murmured. "It would drive me mad in a week. I suppose it is romantic but for romance one needs a man."

"There's George," Antonia reminded her. On the far side of the room she was unpacking her suitcase.

"Oh, God, George! The poor silly man. He does nothing but talk of your friend, Dee."

Antonia paused, looking towards the window. "He worries about her disappearance?"

"Not particularly. Like me, he remembers other happier days."

Antonia returned to her unpacking. "Why don't you tell Roger? That that is what you talk about, I mean."

"Because it would make no difference." Clare leant farther

out. She took a deep breath. "There really is the most heavenly smell. I wonder what it is?"

"The sweet briar hedge, I expect," Antonia answered. So it is true, she reflected. Clare doesn't care for Roger. Keith's death isn't going to bring them together. She did not know whether she was glad or sorry.

She closed the door on the last of her things. She joined Clare at the window, marvelling at the ease with which she could see. The moonlight drifted across the lawns, then gave up at the edge of the woods. It was very silent.

From somewhere in the grounds a car started up.

Antonia's heart seemed to stop. For a moment she stood still, stricken by a sense of unreality. Of horror lurking just beyond her line of vision. Then, with an inarticulate cry she drew in her head and raced for the door.

Clare moved too, swiftly, but with the careful precision of a cat. "What is it?" she cried, following on Antonia's heels. "What's happening?"

"The Bug," Antonia called back, as she raced along the passage. "It's the Bug. Dee's car."

The sitting-room door opened. Mirabella came out, borne, it seemed, on the tide of Mozart's *Requiem*. She was carrying the used coffee things on a tray. She paused staring. "What is happening? Have you two set the house on fire?"

"It's the Bug. It must have been in the car park all the time." Antonia had halted perforce, since Mirabella and the tray filled the passage. A great anguish came over her. "It doesn't seem possible that I passed it and didn't know."

Mirabella turned colour. "It can't be the Bug. It is probably some car on its way to the Home Farm."

Antonia dodged round her. "I'd know that sound anywhere," she declared, tearing open the outer door. Clare followed her out.

"I'll get Sebastian to ring the police," Mirabella called after them.

The two girls paused listening. "This way," Clare called. They ran on into the scented air. Their shadows streamed behind them. And in the distance the Bug banged and chattered its way through the woods.

They came to the trees. Here, the moon struck down only in odd confusing shafts. They stumbled on the rough ground. Brambles impeded their steps. Old rabbit holes threatened to throw them down.

Antonia was scarcely aware of any of this. Mentally she was in the car park. Fearfully she conjured up each tarpaulin-shrouded shape. Had this been Dee's car? Or that? Had the fowls roosted on it, not knowing it for the ghostly thing it was? The dancers laughed and talked around it, not realising—? And had she herself passed it by unknowingly? In her heart she did not believe that she could have done so.

For a moment she had a wild hope that it was Dee driving the Bug, although why or where to she could not imagine.

They came to the cart track. It was easier going here. They saw the light of a torch coming towards them. Behind loomed the large friendly figure of the Chief Inspector. The sound of the car's engine was still audible but drawing farther and farther away.

"We're chasing the Bug," Antonia gasped.

"I thought you might be," Finch answered. "Come on."

Clare's long legs could keep up with him. Small Antonia, for all her determination, would have fallen behind had not her two companions taken her by the arm and pulled her along.

The erratic sound ceased suddenly. For a moment the silence, by contrast, seemed complete. The three pursuers came to a halt.

"It's stopped," cried Antonia excitedly. They waited. When the girl spoke again there was in her voice the echo of a lost hope. "The driver isn't coming this way?"

Clare looked at her swiftly. "It wasn't Dee, love. It couldn't have been."

Antonia sighed desolately. "I know that really. Only somehow I just can't believe it."

"When the car went off the track," said Finch, "the sound seemed to me to veer to the right-hand side. That is, the side of the path farthest from Hone Court." Clare nodded her agreement. "Right, then we'll concentrate on that. We must all three look out for any sign of the car having turned off. Broken branches, twigs, flattened bracken. Anything like that."

They moved on slowly, the light going with them. They had progressed some way when they heard someone coming towards them through the trees. It was Sebastian Chant.

He threw up his arm to protect his eyes. "Turn that damn' thing off, whoever you are," he shouted. And then as he drew nearer: "Oh, it's you." He looked as if he had been walking blindly. His shoes and stockings were sodden and stuck with grass and burrs. His shirt was torn in one place. A smear of mud decorated his forehead. When he spoke it was in the high, petulant voice of inner tension.

"What the devil's happening this evening? Will someone tell me. People everywhere. Someone driving a car. Fella dodging about. This is private property. Not a safari park."

"What fellow was this?" Finch asked. He had switched off his torch and his eyes were beginning to accustom themselves to the tenuous moonlight.

"How should I know?" Sebastian retorted. "I was just standing about thinking when suddenly he appeared. I was going to shout to him but it didn't seem worthwhile."

"Did you see the car?"

"No. Sounded like an old banger. If the dancers had been here I would have thought it was one of theirs."

"How long was this before you met us?"

"Difficult to say. Two or three minutes perhaps."

"We were trying to catch up with the car. D'you think you can find the place where you saw this man? He was probably the driver."

"I can find it all right. Seems a dashed funny thing to do but I can do it. It wasn't far from this track but I'd do better retracing my steps. Don't want the torch though. One's eyes get used to the moonlight." He turned and trudged back into the trees, the others following.

"You've been in the water," Finch commented.

"I walked through the stream," Sebastian answered indifferently. "It was less trouble than jumping and I wasn't near any of the steppingstones."

"This fellow you saw, what did he look like?" Finch asked.

"I didn't see his face." Sebastian, who had been leading the way, halted. "That's queer. Come to think of it the fella didn't have any face. He was just a column of—of, well—shadow. Dark all over. Don't think I'd have noticed him at all if he hadn't been moving."

"A mask of some sort over his face, I suppose." Finch added, "Did you get any impression of age? Height?"

"He was tall. Taller than me anyway. He moved lightly and, once he'd seen me, pretty fast."

Sebastian had resumed walking. He was peering about him. "Know these woods like the palm of my hand." It was, considering the state of his clothes, an odd assertion. He seemed to feel this. He laughed shortly. "I should have said I know them when I think about it. Tonight I wasn't thinking. Not about that. Kept thinking of that poor kid. Same in the house. Only there my wife was making the place unbearable with her music. I don't mind 'Sheep May Safely Graze.' I can just about stand 'Ode to Saint Cecilia,' but when it comes to Mozart's *Requiem* I've had it." He sighed. "Ought to have been more sympathetic, I suppose. Mirabella only plays 'em when she's upset."

The three of them walked on. Far longer than two or three minutes had passed. Finch was beginning to think that their guide was wilfully misleading them when he stopped.

"It was somewhere about here. Yes, I was standing here. The fella appeared through a gap in those hazel bushes. Disappeared"—Sebastian waved a podgy hand—"in that direction."

Finch, as he gazed at the screening bushes, was aware of a deepening sadness. He was in little doubt as to what he would find on the farther side. The two girls stood staring. For them too all sense of adventure had gone, while horror and apprehension remained. Only Sebastian seemed unaffected. He was brushing himself down with his hands, exploring the surface of his shirt for tears.

Finch pushed through the bushes farther up from where

Sebastian had said the man had appeared. He switched on his torch. The light leapt forward across a small enclosed clearing.

In its centre, its bonnet pointing his way, with old-fashioned brass lamps gleaming and soft hood up, stood a roomy two-seater. In spite of the hour and the place where it rested, it contrived to look homely, vaguely dignified and not at all sinister.

Sebastian had followed the others without much interest. Now he came to an abrupt halt. "It's the Bug," he cried in tones of utter stupefaction. "It's the Bug."

"Wait here," said Finch. He walked forward alone.

The two girls stared after him in stricken silence. Clare hugged herself as if some icy wind bit into her bones. Antonia had begun to shake. She knew now, with utter certainty, that when this big man turned back someone, whom she had until then managed to think of as alive, would be unquestionably and eternally dead.

Finch bent and peered into the front of the car. A handsome blue suitcase was the only thing there. He placed the back of his hand for an instant on the seat of the car. But, if the vanished driver had left a faint warmth behind him, it had dissipated in the night air.

He went to the back of the car. He picked up a stick and thrust it through the handle and applied pressure to the lid of the boot. It was not locked.

He raised it a little way. Very carefully he raised it, braced for he knew not what of violence, horror, and perversion. After a single glance he let it close again. He went back to the others.

He addressed himself to Antonia. "I am sorry," he said gently, "your friend is there—dead." There was, he thought, no satisfactory way of breaking bad news.

"Oh, God!" cried Antonia brokenly.

"How did she die?" Clare demanded. It was, Finch thought, a curious question. Curious, that is, coming from Clare and with such intensity of feeling.

"It isn't possible to say at present," he answered.

Sebastian's face had paled. He shook his head in a helpless way. "Dee dead? Why I've known her all her life."

"Things would certainly be pleasanter if only strangers to us were murdered," Finch commented dryly.

Another thought struck Sebastian. "But where has the Bug been?"

"At a guess—in your car park. It was safe enough there until the dancers had this unexpected invitation. It was safe enough when the dancers left. The driver of the last car out would take it for granted that he was last but one. Coming back though it would be a different matter. To find a car still there—yes, that might well have made the dancers curious. So it had to be moved."

Sebastian sighed and looked at Finch. "I suppose I've done it again—put myself out on a limb."

"It is certainly of little use giving you advice," Finch answered dryly. And then: "I'll stay here. I'd be glad if you three would go back to the house and telephone the Winstead police."

"Mrs. Chant may have already done so," said Antonia dully.

The trio set off. From long custom Sebastian put his arm round Antonia. She was just the right height for him to do so. Then, recalling how unwelcome such attentions might be henceforth, he took it away again as sharply as if her shoulder had been red hot.

The action penetrated Antonia's misery. She looked at Sebastian and saw the shame and unhappiness in his face. She mustered a smile. Then, moving close to him, she slipped her arm trustingly through his. Sebastian was much affected. He produced a large white handkerchief and blew his nose loudly. Clare took his other arm. The trio vanished from Finch's sight.

For a little while he heard their uneven footsteps fading into the distance. Small dry twigs crackling under foot. Pebbles rolling. The faint swish of resistant branches. Then the uncaring silence closed in again. He was alone with the dead girl.

He swept the light from his torch around the small clearing. He saw where the car had been driven in at one side. It was the only place where it could have come in. He noted the screen of hazel bushes, the tall trees above, their drooping branches making a cavern of foliage. It had been a good place in which to hide the Bug seeing how little scope for manoeuvre the murderer had had. It had been his bad luck that the one person who would recognise the Bug's engine from all others, had heard the car being moved.

Finch went back to the car and opened the door of the boot as widely as it would go. Stood there, looking in.

Dee Sumner lay on her side facing the opening. Her knees were drawn up towards her chin. Her face had a dreadful pallor but she looked quite peaceful. Except for a stray strand of hair lying across her cheek her corn-coloured hair lay sleek and smooth. Her great brown eyes, although sunken and dull now that the light of intelligence had gone from them, held no expression of terror. Not even of surprise.

She was wearing a long frock of some thin material. Finch thought it might be lawn. It was exotically patterned in shades of apple green, blue, soft reds, and touches of black. It was neither creased nor torn. She was wearing stockings but no shoes.

There were what looked like bruises on her face and neck. Finch recognised them as being post-mortem staining from where the blood had settled. This suggested that the dead girl had been in the same place and position for several days. Probably since the Thursday evening on which she had disappeared, the airlessness in the boot having done much to preserve her.

At the back of the boot was the food probably bought by Dee on the way down. Tins and jars, a box of marron glacé, a wholemeal loaf, and a carton of milk. The newspaper she had had with her in the London restaurant. And tucked in between her knees and the front of the boot was a pair of high-heeled patent-leather sandals and a handbag.

Very carefully, and since there was no one to stop him, Finch slipped a hand under her shoulders and another under her head. Cautiously he raised her, seeking for signs of violence. As he did so something in the way her head moved roused his suspicions. He took away his hand and the lovely head dropped at an unnatural angle.

So that might account for there being no sign of a struggle having taken place in the cottage, he thought. Someone had struck the girl a single skilful blow from behind. It had broken her neck.

"Whoever did that to you, lady," he said aloud, "was no sex maniac. And anyway it was a damned shame."

He closed the boot of the car reluctantly. He was aware of a totally irrational feeling that the dead girl, who had so much enjoyed living, might not care to be consigned once more to the lonely darkness.

He found the stump of a tree and sat down. A line of Walter de la Mare's was running through his mind:

> Here lies a most beautiful lady
> Light of heart and step was she—

There was nothing in his pleasant and sleepy-looking face to indicate the sick anger and regret he felt. Sex murders were more horrible but at least the perpetrator was driven by an urge he could not control. The killing of Dee Sumner had been cold, ruthless, and calculated.

Finch sat on, trying to make some sense of the two violent deaths. Presently he heard the sound of several cars approaching. He saw their headlights shining through the trees. Flashing his torch he went forward to meet the Winstead police.

Mirabella Chant had been up early. She was always the first to get up in that house. Now she was first in the kitchen. While the eggs and bacon were cooking for her breakfast she stood by the stove looking out of the window.

It was a still day. The sky was colourless. The trees were motionless. Mist trailed thinly across the grass and veiled the far distance.

Mirabella sighed. The day on which the young men had been drowned had begun just like this. It was a sad thought with which to begin the day. She reflected that the same thought might come to Clare and sadden her further. She decided to try and like the girl better.

She wished that she could rid herself of the feeling that

there was something false about the young woman. Or was she only trying to rationalise an illogical dislike?

The door opened. Clare Vesey came in. She looked cool and composed. Plainly, Mirabella reflected, the state of the weather had, as yet, held no particular significance for her. "Good morning," she said, "what sort of night did you both have?"

"Antonia didn't get to sleep until nearly five. She is awake again now."

"Four hours! That isn't enough. And I suppose you got no sleep either?"

Clare smiled—remotely, Mirabella considered. "I can cat-nap almost anywhere." She added: "I came down to get Antonia's breakfast. Cereal, tea, and perhaps a bit of toast?"

"An excellent menu," Mirabella agreed. "I will take it up to her." She began to lay the tray as she spoke.

"I think I should take it. I am the one person in the house whom Antonia doesn't connect with her friend."

There was sense in Clare's words Mirabella admitted, grudgingly. "Give the dear child my love," she said. As she sat down at the table she reflected that perhaps it was this general reasonableness that she found so unlikeable.

Sebastian came in. He greeted Clare. Enquired rather perfunctorily after Antonia and remarked: "I went down to the village to see what news I could pick up. And I must say I was given some pretty queer looks. Shouldn't be surprised if I don't end up a local pariah."

"I suppose everyone is suspect until the murderer is caught," said Clare, deftly removing two pieces of toast from the grill.

Sebastian gave her a sour look. "Only some are more suspect than others." He fell into a gloomy abstraction.

"But what was the news?" Mirabella was at the stove again cooking Sebastian's breakfast. Everyone else had to fend for themselves.

"Eh? Oh, the news! They were saying that Dee had had her neck broken."

"An accident?" Clare was staring at him in disbelief.

"No. Done on purpose."

"Horrible!" cried Mirabella, drawing out the word and screwing her eyes tight shut. "What else?"

"Nothing else."

The eyes flew open. "There must have been."

"I tell you there wasn't. Dee died of a single blow delivered to the back of the neck. She was bunged into the boot of her car—and left in our car park."

"D'you mean," demanded Mirabella, "that there was no struggle?"

"No struggle."

"No sexual assault?"

"None."

Clare smiled faintly. "That should comfort Antonia. She has nearly gone out of her mind imagining all the dreadful ways in which Dee might have died."

"The poor kid," said Sebastian. "That *is* a point to the good."

Mirabella was flicking the fat over Sebastian's eggs with a knife. She did it with sharp, vicious flicks. "But it's all wrong," she burst out. "Here we have been warning Dee for years past. Telling her that she was in danger of getting herself raped and mutilated. Drawing awful pictures of an unavailing fight. Of screams no one would hear. And what happens? She gets herself killed as neatly as if she had been a cashier walking to the bank, with the week's takings."

"It's illogical," Clare agreed, preparing to leave the room with the tray. "But what strikes me as strange is that the local people should know so much so quickly. I suppose the news comes from the local constable. What's his name? Hob something or other."

Sebastian shook his head. "Smoke signals, native drums, or thought transference—but not Hobday. He has too much respect for the law."

Clare went away with the tray. Mirabella placed Sebastian's breakfast in front of him. The telephone rang and she raised her head listening.

"Good! Michael's answering. I suppose it's some newspaper or other. There have been half a dozen on the line already." She added: "Michael didn't get back until twenty to eleven

(123)

last night. I wouldn't have thought Judith wanted all that support."

Michael came into the room. "That was the police. They say they'll be round about half-past ten—if that's all right by Antonia."

Mirabella opened her eyes wide. "What do they want with her."

"They're bringing round the clothes Dee was wearing. They want Antonia to identify them."

Abruptly Sebastian pushed back his plate. He looked sick. "Don't think I can manage eggs and bacon this morning," he said miserably.

Mirabella patted his hand. "You're a good man, Sebastian," she declared. "A good, sweet man."

Sebastian looked alarmed. "Don't you go saying that to the police," he cried. "They'd clap me in jail for certain." He looked at her with foreboding. In general he considered himself fortunate in his marriage—but not on occasions such as this.

NINE

It was a quarter to ten. Septimus Finch was coming to the end of a leisurely and hearty breakfast, taken in a dining room that was otherwise empty. Most people had breakfasted early and were now upstairs packing. Two murders and the killer still at large had been too much for their nerves. They were waiting only to be interviewed by the police before leaving for home.

Since the police had started their activities at first light, Finch reflected, they would no doubt get to the Bull's Head some time that day—but certainly not as soon as expected.

He himself had had no part in the police activities or deliberations. This had not surprised him. He had recognised as a declaration of policy Bollard's assertion that he, Finch, was to be that most modern and useful of adjuncts, a think tank. And one to work strictly in the background, although this the Superintendent had not actually said. It had not depressed Finch—although the outcome he considered might well depress Bollard.

When it was known that the Yard man was in the district— and it would be known, for his was a familiar face and figure to crime reporters—the Superintendent would feel forced by the weight of public opinion to seek him out, Bollard being in Finch's opinion far too sensitive to pressure of that kind.

However, since that time was not yet, he was a little surprised to see Ben Engleman peering through the glass doors of the dining room. He saw Finch and came across the floor. He looked with some respect at the remains of his friend's breakfast. "I had no idea they did you so well at the Bull's Head," he remarked.

"Since one of the staff recognised me I have become an object of veneration," said Finch blandly. "They keep coming and peering in at me. Even the manager has had a look. I don't mind as long as they don't touch the exhibit." He added: "Get yourself a cup from the side table and have some coffee. I've just had a second lot made." He watched Ben cross the room and wondered what he—or rather the Superintendent—wanted.

When Engleman had returned he remarked amiably: "See anything of the press?"

"They're beginning to swarm," Engleman answered gloomily. "Shouldn't be surprised if we weren't soon forced to divert men to keep a watch out for them. Mrs. Harker or the Chants are sure to complain."

"I shouldn't worry too much about that. By the look of the weather my guess is that the whole place will be lost in fog by four o'clock. That should baffle them."

"That's all this business needs—fog," said Engleman disgustedly. He brightened slightly. "It might prevent the parents of those young men who were drowned from flying back to this country. We traced the Prices to Persia and the Greenwoods to Italy. The Lynhams have only to get here by train from London. Greengrocers in a small way—and I bet they didn't see much of their daughter either."

"Nothing startling to be expected from the inquest?"

"Nothing, thank Heavens! It appears that there was some surprise that the body of David Price took so long to come ashore but it seems to have had no particular significance. Like the other two, he was drowned in the sea. Such injuries as he sustained were, like theirs, inflicted after death, the work of fish, rock, or water."

Finch nodded. "Have you had time to see the newspapers? They're doing the murders proud. I wonder if the murderer realised just what a furore he was going to cause when he decided to kill Dee Sumner."

"Decided, is the operative word. The fact that he wasn't a sex maniac seems to turn the case upside down," Engleman complained. "Without McKnight's brain storm theory we can't even explain why all that polishing took place at the Thatched Cottage. Unless the chap was just overcautious."

Finch shook his head. "There must be some explanation but it's not that." He sat back in his chair. His forehead was creased. "Another queer thing to my mind is the time lag. Dee Sumner presumably was murdered on the Thursday. Yet the second girl, Beatrice Lynham, waited until Sunday to make that fatal appointment."

Ben grinned. "The same thought occurred to McKnight. He suggests a commercial traveller."

Finch chuckled. "Here Thursday. Back again Sunday. Could be."

"But not likely." Engleman added: "We found the place where the first girl was killed. It was farther away from where Mr. Chant saw her and a good bit nearer the Limes."

Finch gave him a questioning look. "From *where* he saw her? You believe his story then?"

Engleman looked dubious. "Only thing that makes us doubt him is that he could have been the driver of the car last night. He would have known that Miss Hughes would recognise the sound of the Bug. On the other hand, when he left the sitting room both girls were listening to music and didn't look like moving."

"Music which he says drove him out of the house," Finch pointed out. "I was inclined at the time to believe him."

"He certainly carried out all the actions he said he did earlier that evening. And the young couple, whom he mentioned, came forward as soon as they heard of the murders. They said that they saw him, 'hot, pink and bothered'—their own description—floundering about in the bracken. Before they actually saw him they heard him calling 'Beatrice, where the devil are you?' They thought Beatrice must be a dog that had gone off hunting.

"Then again his story made it easy for us to find the actual scene of the murder—where the grass and bracken had been trampled down. We could follow the murderer's progress to the Limes too. He had knotted the girl's sash at the back and used it as a handle." Engleman added savagely: "Must have made it dead easy for him to heave her over the fence into the garden of the Limes.

Finch nodded. "He's a cold-blooded fellow right enough."

"The forensic people found a few rhododendron leaves and a twig from a dwarf Japanese maple caught up on the frill at the hem of her frock. There was only one place in the garden where the two grew close together. And from there the murderer could see, not the front door but the drive, so that he could watch for Mrs. Harker to leave—that is if the killer wasn't Mrs. Harker."

"Which it might have been?"

"We haven't a clue really. We interviewed the young man who sat next to Beatrice Lynham at lunch yesterday. He described her as excited and a bit above herself. As if"—Engleman made a slight grimace—"something nice was going to happen. He said too that she was always making extravagant claims, like saying she could make Sebastian Chant do anything she wanted—even marry her."

Finch helped himself to another piece of toast. "I trust that doesn't mean that your Superintendent harbours any ill intentions towards Mrs. Chant? Mirabella is quite my favourite screwball."

"Could be either of the young men I suppose. As you know, Miss Lynham had been pretty thick with Keith Vesey and that meant she must have seen a lot of Roger Frampton as well. Anyway, we got round to Frampton latish yesterday evening and his alibi wasn't all that convincing. He was in the village doing a bit of shopping somewhere about the time of the murder. After that he was alone at Treadle Bay Cottage. He was there again alone when Hobday went round to the cottage about eleven-thirty yesterday evening, after the discovery of the second body. He said he hadn't been out but we only have his word for it."

"What time did Michael Chant get back to Hone Court?"

"About twenty to eleven. He and Mrs. Harker alibied each other but from the amount of drink she'd had that evening I doubt if she had a very clear picture of where he was or what was going on."

"None of the alibis can be said to be impressive," Finch remarked.

"Don't I know it," Engleman groaned. "You'd think a girl as smart as Beatrice Lynham was said to have been would have had more sense than to make an appointment with a murderer in the middle of a wood."

"She probably did make the appointment to meet in some more public place."

"Then how—?"

"Turn it the other way round. The murderer agrees to meet her where she says—teashop? The crowded beach? He's not worried because he counts on her doing just what she does do. Walks to their rendezvous through the woods."

"You mean he waylaid her?"

"What do you think?" Finch asked with a certain complacence.

Engleman sighed. "We had no joy with the second murder either. We began a search of the woods at first light. Police from all over the county, metal detectors and tracker dogs. For a start, the driver of the car fooled the dogs by walking down the stream. Probably had a bicycle hidden somewhere nearby. There are literally dozens of them in a big barn at Hone Court."

"I know. I saw them when I was looking for the car park. Half of them looked ready for the junk yard. I don't suppose anyone could tell if half a dozen were missing."

"Just what Mr. Chant said," said Engleman gloomily.

"How about the p.m. on Dee Sumner?"

"Dr. Haynes reported that she was a fine girl physically. That all organs were in good condition. That she died from a single karate blow to the back of the neck. Died within half an hour of eating bread, butter, honey, and an apple. That puts the probable time of death at seven-thirty or a little later. There were no signs of physical assault. He said too that the girl had had no recent sexual intercourse."

Both Finch's eyebrows climbed. "That's odd."

"The Superintendent thinks the explanation is that Mrs. Harker was responsible for both murders. It's making him pretty unbearable."

Finch nodded. "I can imagine." He added: "You did mention a curious find?"

"That was P. C. Craddock's discovery. He was following the course of the stream at the time and there it was. Trampled plants, a half-hidden footprint and, impaled on a thornbush, this bit of silk." As Engleman spoke he produced an envelope and shook from it a scrap of material. It was pennant shape, roughly torn and ragged at the edges. It was about five inches long and some three inches across.

Finch picked it up. "Pure silk," he commented. "Expensive. A distinctive design too."

"I can see that, thanks," Engleman retorted. "Craddock also found that, at one point, the ground was littered with dead twigs and branches. And that it looked as if something heavy had been dragged through the bushes. He concluded, not unnaturally, that this was the scene of Miss Sumner's murder."

Finch stared. "Not unnaturally? My dear Ben!"

Engleman looked stubborn. "I'm told it looks exactly as if a struggle had taken place there."

Finch shook his head. "No struggle."

"That's what it looks like—a struggle."

"In that frock? Never."

Engleman was silent for a moment. "I can't say that I'm altogether satisfied," he admitted. "But I must be off. I'm going there now."

Finch sighed. "You're so hasty."

"Well, there is something you can do if you will. Superintendent Bollard would be glad if you would go with McKnight to Hone Court with the clothes Dee Sumner was wearing. Ask Miss Hughes to identify them. I had made an appointment for half-past ten." He grinned suddenly. "As a matter of fact, Miss Hughes refused to see anyone else. Bollard is quite put out."

"My heart bleeds for him," Finch murmured. And then: "How about the things in the boot of the car?"

"I imagine that everything Miss Sumner brought down with her was there—bar her keys. No clues though."

"A pity." Finch commandeered the bit of silk so that he could show it to Antonia. He stipulated too that he should be allowed to examine the contents of Dee's suitcase.

Hobday's house was now more police station than home. It was a place of ordered bustle, of messages taken and answered, of telephones ringing and people calling, some with information. Some with complaints and demands that they be allowed to leave Hone.

McKnight was at the front door looking out for Finch. He took him into what had been the Hobdays' sitting room.

"Mrs. Hobday being the old-fashioned sort," he explained, "she'd never dream of putting her own wishes before those of her husband's superiors."

As he spoke McKnight was putting the dead girl's suitcase on the centre table, where Finch could, more comfortably, see what it contained. The clothes she had been wearing at the time of her murder made a small pile—scandalously small, Mrs. Hobday considered—beside it.

McKnight watched Finch's examination with melancholy eyes. "She was a doll—a real doll," he said sadly. "To die as she did doesn't make sense." He was unaware that with these sentiments Mirabella Chant was in complete agreement.

A police constable hurried in. He glanced curiously at Finch before he spoke. "Mr. Harker's in the passage outside, Sarge. Says he thought he'd find the Super here."

"Show him in." McKnight glanced at Finch. "You'd like to speak to him no doubt, sir. And, Dawson, get this suitcase and the clothes out to the car—pronto."

George Harker appeared to have reacted violently to the news of Dee's murder. His eyes were stricken. His face was a sickly grey.

McKnight explained the position to their visitor. He introduced Finch.

"It doesn't really matter who I speak to," said Harker. "I asked for the Superintendent because I knew him. That was all." As he spoke he walked over to the window and stood staring blindly out.

"You had something to tell us?" Finch prompted.

Harker turned. He smiled in a rather savage manner. "I realise, of course, that you must suspect me of killing Dee—Miss Sumner. Since I didn't do it that doesn't worry me. What does get me is that, on Thursday, I heard the murderer—and I did nothing towards getting my hands on him."

McKnight gave him a quick, startled glance.

"Tell me about it," Finch invited in his soft voice.

"I knew that Miss Sumner was coming down here on the Thursday, got it from the night porter at the block of flats. I'd been intending for some time to go to the States on business. Trouble was I couldn't make up my mind to cut my losses —until this week when it became imperative that I went." He spoke in a dry, brittle voice, a lifeless voice. In short sentences and words that dried up and fell into silence.

"So you decided to see Miss Sumner for the last time," Finch prompted.

"That's it. Meant to say good-bye. I thought perhaps she'd come with me—just for the fun of the thing." George sighed. "Didn't really think it. Knew she was through with me—but I went just the same."

George was silent a moment. Pursuing some barren, unprofitable road of his own. "I didn't hurry down," he said at last. "Stopped to have a meal in Maidstone. Where? A restaurant on the main road. Don't remember its name. The food wasn't bad but the service was lousy and the dining room overcrowded. I fancy there had been some do in the town. I arrived at Hone about nine. Parked the car on the bit of waste land near the sea and had a look in the various pubs. She wasn't there so I walked to the Thatched Cottage.

"Place was in darkness. Didn't surprise me. Thought Dee would be home sometime. Sat down on the seat in the porch to wait. It was very quiet. Remember an owl came out of the woods and floated over the fields. Lovely sight. Perhaps a bit eerie. The young fellow from the farm passed with his girl. Sounded happy."

Again there came that painful silence. George rubbed his eyes wearily. He resumed abruptly. "Suddenly I heard someone walking briskly and lightly towards the cottage through the woods. I stepped out of the porch and walked round the cottage in the direction of the sound."

"And then?" Finch prompted him. He was thinking that George Harker too had, albeit unwittingly, kept vigil over the dead girl.

"The footsteps ceased. After a moment I said, 'That you, Dee?' Although I knew very well it wasn't. She would have come to the hedge, if only to damn my eyes for following her about. No one answered. After a moment I heard the footsteps again. Only this time they were moving away—back into the woods —carefully now, and furtively. I shouted, 'Hi! Come back here!' " George had been staring blankly, reliving the moment. Now he looked at Finch. "Wanted to get my hands on him. Thought he was Dee's lover. I'd have gone after him, only the hedge was too high. I could only stand and curse."

"From which direction did the footsteps come?"

"It's a bit difficult to say. I heard him because he had stepped off the path. He had to push his way through the undergrowth. At the time I thought he was walking parallel with the hedge but some way in. Meaning to come out into the lane by the garage."

"And when he withdrew?"

"The same thing. Heard him until he got to the path. Got the idea though that he hadn't gone farther. Was waiting there for me to go—which I did."

So that was twice the murderer had escaped the risk of detection because he had been thought to be Dee's lover. Finch supposed that there was a certain bleak humour about this.

Personally he had no heart to appreciate it. "What time was it when you left the cottage?"

"I wasn't bothering about the time. But when I was getting into the car I heard the church clock strike ten. I had been walking fast. Couldn't have taken me more than ten minutes to get there." George hesitated, his head bent. Then, without raising his head, but with a hard heavy regard he looked at Finch. "Is it true that, while I sat outside, Dee was inside the cottage, dead?"

Finch nodded. "We think she died about half-past seven. When you heard the murderer he was coming back to clear up."

George was silent a moment while his eyes seemed to explore the cheerful pattern of Mrs. McKnight's carpet. Then he said —but more as if he were talking to himself: "When I catch up with the bastard I'll tear him apart."

When Finch and McKnight were in the police car the sergeant said in his precise way, "We had already had two people come in this morning. Both had noticed the Maserati parked near the beach. They reported it because they knew Mr. Harker drove one and knew of his association with Miss Sumner."

The double gates leading to the grounds of Hone Court were closed. Two uniformed constables stood on guard. Facing them was a little group of sensation hunters and a few press men representing national newspapers.

Finch's appearance caused a sensation among these latter. They showed renewed signs of attempting to storm the gates. Foiled in this by the two policemen they shouted comments and questions. In response Finch raised one hand in a vaguely benedictory gesture. This, as the police car passed through the gateway, was greeted with a half-derisive cheer.

Michael opened the door at Hone Court. He showed the two detectives into the drawing room, remarking formally that Miss Hughes was expecting them.

In proof of this Antonia came in a minute later, accompanied by Mirabella. Her face was paper white with great dark smudges under her eyes but she was calm. Too much so. Finch thought that she was in a mild state of shock.

"I'm glad it's you," Antonia said, giving him her hand. "A friend. It makes it less unbearable." Her voice died on the last word as if fatigue had taken the very sound from her lips.

Finch looked at her with a good deal of kindness. "By now I expect you have heard how Miss Sumner died. It has been confirmed by the police surgeon. He says it is unlikely that she saw the blow coming. Or even realised that she was in danger. So there would have been no fear, no long-drawn agony."

Antonia had listened with an alarmed painful intensity. Yet for a moment the sense of his words didn't seem to penetrate. It was Mirabella who spoke.

"Extra-or-dinary! I can't see how it happened like that. To my mind it makes no sense."

"Just what I said, ma'am," said McKnight.

Antonia expelled a long breath. "I have had such awful thoughts—even asleep."

"We all have," Mirabella declared, pursing and unpursing her lips.

McKnight had unwrapped the parcel and laid its contents on the centre table. From another bag he took the high-heeled patent-leather sandals.

Antonia looked at the little collection sadly. "Yes, those are Dee's. The pantie-girdle and bra were made to match for her by—" She named an exclusive West End shop. "The frock was one I chose for her. At least, when I saw the sketch I realised how wonderful she would look in it."

"It seems a rather elaborate frock to bring down here," Finch said gently.

"Dee always brought one fabulous outfit with her," Antonia answered, "in case she met someone it was worth dressing up for."

And all that had happened this time was that she had got herself murdered in it, Finch reflected. For if it hadn't been lover-boy who had killed Dee why hadn't he come forward and said so?

He remarked aloud: "One other point. D'you happen to remember what shoes your friend was wearing when she left London?"

Antonia frowned in an effort to remember. "I can only recall the bag," she said at last. "That was black leather. So obviously her shoes would have been leather too. They'd have been court shoes—with low heels. Dee didn't like high heels with trousers except in the evening."

"There are none like that in her suitcase. They may be at the Thatched Cottage. Would you mind coming with us and seeing if you can identify them?"

"Now?"

"When you have seen this." Finch took an envelope from an inner pocket. From it he took the scrap of silk found in the woods explaining how and where it had been found. He passed it to Antonia.

Her expression changed. She cried out in horror. Stepping back involuntarily she let the scrap of gaily patterned silk float down to the floor.

Mirabella started up. "Antonia! What is it?"

The girl was staring at the bit of silk as if it held some terrible message for her. "George Harker," she whispered, "that is a piece of silk torn from one of his scarves." She began to tremble.

Mirabella gave an exclamation. "Impossible."

Finch glanced at her. "Why do you say that?"

"Why?" Mirabella looked rather wildly around as if for the answer. Then she said firmly: "Because George was devoted to Dee. Quite devoted—and in the nicest possible way."

Finch stooped and retrieved the scrap. "It's distinctive enough to be recognisable. Bright green background, black zig-zag strokes, and small white globes. When had you seen it before, Miss Hughes?"

"Last summer. Yes, just over a year ago. It was the end of August and Mr. Harker was wearing a scarf with that pattern. When I admired the colouring he took it off and gave it to me to look at. He said it belonged to some polo club he used to play for. The green represented the grass. The white blobs were the balls and the black strokes their flight."

This seemed sufficient identification for Finch. Mirabella was not satisfied. "Are you certain they are not tennis balls?

That would be a really trendy idea." She added positively: "Yes, I feel certain that they are tennis balls."

"Trendy things aren't made in this quality," Antonia said. "I know fabrics. This scarf must have been really expensive. The luxury trade."

Finch nodded. "Thank you. That's what I thought." He put the scrap of silk back in its envelope. "And now, Miss Hughes, if you'd come back to the Thatched Cottage and look at the shoes. We have a car outside."

Clare was standing in the hall, looking from the window. She turned smiling encouragingly at Antonia.

Finch greeted her. Then he asked Mirabella whether she wished to accompany Antonia.

Mirabella shook her head. "The Winstead police are here questioning the dancers. I must stay on their account. Who knows what may come of it? *Habeas corpus?* Bail? Who can say?"

"Then perhaps Clare—?" Antonia faltered.

"Of course I'll come, love. Then perhaps afterwards you'll walk with me over the downs. The fresh air will do us good."

"Your husband is out?" Finch asked Mirabella.

Mirabella, who had been scowling at Clare's back (why did she have to push herself forward?), turned and said severely: "For the first time since our marriage my husband is cleaning his father's guns. He declares he will pepper the first newspaper reporter who gets into the house."

"That will be no solution, ma'am," said McKnight disapprovingly.

Mirabella drew herself up. "We leave the solution to you, sergeant," she declaimed superbly. "We provide ourselves merely with a *divertissement.*"

At Finch's suggestion the police car left the Court by the back drive to miss the reporters. It wasn't until they were passing through the lodge gates that McKnight spoke. "It's certainly been an experience meeting that lady, sir," he remarked, alluding to Mrs. Chant.

At the cottage he stayed downstairs talking to the constable who told him that there had been no disturbance that night and no unknown visitor. Finch followed the two girls up to Dee's bedroom.

While Clare stared about her curiously Antonia crouched down in front of the shoe cupboard. She opened the double doors. "Dee had a thing about shoes," she remarked, sitting back on her heels in front of it. "Have you any idea how many pairs there are here?"

Finch said no, but he had. An awed McKnight had told him. Thirty-eight pairs he'd said. All on racks and all looking as if they had just come out of the shop.

"There are thirty-eight pairs here and dozens more in London," Antonia said, adding: "At least, there should be thirty-eight."

She and Finch counted them. Thirty-eight was the number. Antonia began to examine them, taking out one pair after another. "These," she suggested, holding them out.

"You're sure?"

Antonia shook her head. "It's just that these would have gone with the handbag." She selected another pair. "It could equally well have been these." Adding: "Why must you know?"

"We don't want to waste time searching for the shoes if they are already here."

Antonia looked up at him helplessly. "I can't be certain."

They all three went downstairs.

The two sheets of paper left by Mrs. Epps still lay on the oak chest. Antonia took them up. "I suppose I had better walk down and pay this. Poor Mrs. Epps! She adored Dee but she never could accept her untidiness—" Abruptly she broke off what she was saying. "Oh!" she exclaimed sharply. And then in a voice of utmost conviction, "That must have been what he was looking for that night—the shoes."

"What shoes?"

"The shoes that were on the oak chest. I think now that, by some freak chance, Dee must have picked up her shoes and put them there." Antonia looked at Finch with distressed eyes. "I carried them up to my bedroom to get them out of the way so I must have blurred any fingerprints."

Finch was conscious of a sudden conviction that he was about

(138)

to strike pay dirt. "If the shoes were so important to your night visitor they must be important to us," he declared.

"I'll get them."

"We'll come with you."

The three of them hurried up the second staircase to Antonia's room. The shoes stood neatly side by side in the bottom of her wardrobe. A sling-back pair, plain, narrow and low heeled. Elegant because they had been expensive.

"How did you carry them?"

"By the strap at the back I expect," adding dolefully, "I wasn't being careful or anything like that." It seemed incredible now that she should have treated them with so little regard.

Finch asked for two plastic bags. Antonia provided them by emptying out a couple of woolly sweaters. Lifting the shoes with the aid of a steel file borrowed from the dressing table he dropped them carefully, one into each bag. "You realise," he said in his soft voice, "that since the finding of the Bug, the character of the enquiry has changed? A sex murder is something that just happens. This was different. It was a cold, calculated killing with a definite motive behind it."

"I had realised that." Antonia pushed her hair back from her face with an almost frantic gesture. "Last night I thought and thought but I couldn't think of any possible reason."

"Who gets your friend's estate?" Finch asked.

"Some charity. I forget which. Dee's parents left it like that in their will."

"And the trustees?"

"The family solicitor and some old friend of Dee's father."

"Mr. Chant perhaps?"

Antonia shook her head. "Oh, no. I can't imagine anyone making Sebastian a trustee. I mean, he's not exactly a financial wizard."

"I suppose your friend couldn't have been married secretly?"

"I feel certain she wasn't. Dee always said that unless she fell deeply in love like her father, she'd stay single."

"A very sensible resolve," Finch observed. And made a mental note to pursue this line of enquiry. "D'you think it possible that she might have learnt a business secret from some tycoon.

Industrial espionage perhaps? A merger? I imagine Miss Sumner was not the most discreet of young women."

"Only because she had no guile," Antonia protested. "And even then, since business didn't interest her, she would have forgotten what was said almost at once."

"Unless," said Finch, "it was something so important—so far reaching—" He considered his own suggestion then shook his head. "No. Somehow I can only see her forgetting the whole thing." He considered a moment. "I suppose she didn't carry anything valuable about on her person?"

Antonia smiled faintly. "A fabulous jewel given her by a South American millionaire? No, Dee was no golddigger." She recalled the scrap of silk with a shudder. "Could George Harker have killed her?"

"He could have done—but somehow I don't think he did."

Clare spoke for the first time. "At least the dancers are above suspicion."

"I suppose one of them could have come back and killed Beatrice," suggested Antonia distastefully.

Clare's lips curled. "True—but what would any of them have to offer a girl like Beatrice Lynham?"

Finch nodded. Clare had something there.

TEN

As the day progressed Hone became transformed by the arrival of sightseers and sensation hunters. Cars were parked everywhere. Little knots of people stared and speculated and, in many cases, were moved on by the police.

They poured into the shops and roamed the woods trying, mostly unsuccessfully, to identify the exact spot where Beatrice Lynham had been strangled and where the old two-seater with its ghastly cargo had been found. In the space of a few hours the Thatched Cottage, the Limes, and Hone Court became temporarily as familiar by name as the Taj Mahal and Buckingham Palace.

Almost everyone was interrogated. Romance blossomed posthumously between Keith and Beatrice. A thin straggling line of people climbed the downs to stare at the Race Rocks or picnic on the springy turf within sight of them.

It was, Sebastian complained, like living in a goldfish bowl. In retaliation he had loosed off an old muzzle loader that had belonged to his grandfather. This caused astonishment, dismay, and even some terror. It also caused Sebastian to take a more favourable view of his sporting ancestors.

About twelve o'clock there was an exodus of newspapermen.

Superintendent Bollard was giving a press conference in Winstead. Life for everyone became far less difficult. Even Finch, still at the cottage, had no more to put up with than the occasional attempt of some brash personage to get past the police guard.

Engleman, returning from the woods, went in search of his friend. He hurried up the cottage path. The police constable saw him coming and opened the front door. He was sent to move on the growing group of sightseers staring in over the garden gate.

"Come in, Ben," Finch welcomed him. "It's still amazingly quiet."

"The Super," Engleman explained, "always spreads himself at a press conference. He likes them to have impact. He usually finishes up by hinting at a dramatic development about which his lips are sealed for the moment."

Finch stared. "A bit risky of him, isn't it?"

"Possibly. The local press have learnt to discount his predictions. They've had to." Although Engleman did not know it this time the Superintendent's dramatic development was drawing momentously nearer, borne by Detective Sergeant McKnight.

Engleman pulled up a chair. "I'm worried, Septimus. Yes, now I've seen the place Craddock came upon, I'm worried. It looks exactly as if a terrific struggle had taken place there." He stared uneasily at his friend.

Finch raised an eyebrow. "The murder that never was?"

Engleman laughed shortly. "Or the murder that hasn't yet come to light. Damn it, Septimus, it's like a bad dream."

"I must admit, Ben," said Finch soberly, "that I'm beginning to be conscious of an utterly unexplained element in this case. The presence of someone who has not, so far, materialised."

"Materialised? You make it sound like a ghost." Engleman sprang to his feet. "Come and look at this discovery of Craddock's. I'd like your opinion. Mine is beginning to frighten me."

Finch followed him from the cottage. "You have someone brooding over the spot I trust?"

"Yes, fellow called Samuels. He has strict orders not to leave his post."

The woods surrounding Hone Court had lost all their mystery by day. They were merely extensive and overgrown. The track through them was rutted and uneven. The police car bounced from one pothole to the next and Engleman swore.

The car stopped. Finch got out and looked about him. "It must have been just about here I saw Sebastian Chant last night."

"Very possibly. The Bug was found on the far side of the track. We're making for a spot on the opposite side, nearer to Hone Court."

Engleman plunged into the woods. Paused to get his bearings, then hurried on once more. They came to the stream and he turned to follow its course. "We've had what may be a bit of luck," he remarked. "We've found a garage hand in Winstead who remembers filling up Miss Sumner's petrol tank. He says there was a dark young man with her in the car but that he didn't notice him much. Says who would with a girl like that to look at."

"He had something there, Ben."

"Maybe. Anyway, we're bringing him over to look at both Michael Chant and Roger Frampton. The sight of one of them may refresh his memory."

The trees were growing close together. The stream had widened to form a pool. There were a few mossy rocks and the sunlight failed to penetrate the thick canopy of leaves.

"A very suitable place for murder," Finch commented politely.

"It gets even more suitable farther on," Engleman retorted. "I'm following the course of the stream only because otherwise it is difficult to find."

"Craddock found it," Finch pointed out, thinking this significant.

"Only because he was doing what I'm doing—following the stream."

The undergrowth thickened. Engleman, with Finch following, pushed his way through a tunnel of intertwined and leafy bushes. They emerged suddenly into a small shadowy and secretive space, full of a thick green gloom. It was enclosed by straggling and decaying evergreens. Tall trees drooped dark branches overhead and the stream, as if yielding to the general mood, ran green and dark and full of broken images.

It was a sinister-looking place. Doubly sinister because, except for themselves, it was empty.

"Samuels," cried Engleman blankly. "He's gone."

It was very silent now in the enclosed space. So silent that the two men could hear the stream like a voice whispering past. Hear too in the distance the sound of music. Music sweet and melodious.

Engleman's face darkened. "Those damned dancers!" He grinned unpleasantly as if pleased at the thought of finding some legitimate object on which to vent his temper. "Come on. If anything has happened to Samuels under cover of that caterwauling I'll make them sorry." He began to force his way through the dusty bushes.

Here the trees were more widely spaced, mainly because many of their number had been felled and carted away. Saplings and bushes had grown up in their place. The music now was clear.

Finch recognised it. "Not caterwauling," he murmured in his small voice, "it's Saint-Saëns's *Le Cygne*."

"Out here? They must be mad."

The music now was close at hand. Engleman parted some obscuring branches. The two men found themselves staring at a most singular sight.

A record-player stood on the grass pouring out the composition that had attracted their attention. The sunlight shone in through a gap in the tall trees, almost like a spotlight.

In the radiance all alone, plump and elderly, Mirabella Chant was performing the dance immortalized by Pavlova. That of the Dying Swan. Her only audience was P. C. Samuels, who peered in a bemused state from a bush almost opposite his enraged superior.

Mirabella was clad from head to foot in a black leotard, under which she protruded in a series of curious bulges. On her head she wore a band, to which adhered a few white feathers. On plump legs, ending in shabby white satin ballet shoes, she glided uncertainly across the rough ground. Her expression was rapt, tranquil, and very sad. She was approaching expiration.

Mirabella's arms—wings—beat now more weakly. Once or twice she faltered. Her movements became slower. She sank to the ground. Her arms coiled like serpents. Her plump body quivered, fell forward. The music ceased. The swan was dead.

Finch had been conscious that Engleman had left his side almost immediately after their arrival. Now he himself turned and hurried after his friend. He could see him in the distance in furious denunciation of the unfortunate Samuels.

They all three forced their way back into the small clearing. Engleman, a ghastly suspicion in his heart, bent to raise the forget-me-not plant.

"There you are, sir," cried Samuels triumphantly. "The footprint is just as I left it."

Finch looked at it with solemn eyes. "It's not, you know. You've been done."

Engleman turned on him fiercely. "What d'you mean? Done? The print is still there."

"But it isn't the same print. This one is broader and the pattern is different."

Suddenly the humour of the situation overcame Finch. Before Engleman's furious gaze and Samuels's hostile one he leant against a tree trunk and collapsed into helpless laughter. Nor was his friend pacified in any way on hearing of the jumbo.

"I suppose Mrs. Chant wanted to distract suspicion from her family," said Finch as the two men fought their way up the stream towards the car. (The unfortunate Samuels—"and don't think you've heard the last of this"—had been ordered to walk back to Hone Police Station.) "Rummaging in the cupboard to find something both anonymous and striking she must have come on the scarf and shoes, the one probably pushed into the other to indicate that both belonged to the same person."

The two men had left the stream now and were walking through the woods. "You must agree, Ben, that, in a way, you have had your revenge. Just consider the perfectly horrible morning Mirabella must have spent. Up at first light setting the stage for a scene of rape, violence, and murder, to find later that only the last of these had taken place. Later still she learns that the clues she had planted would lead us straight to a man already suspected. One clue, she must have realised was irretrievably lost—even to one of her ingenuity—but the second could still be obliterated."

Engleman was not appeased. "I suppose that is where her husband came in."

Finch shook his head. "I fancy that over the years Sebastian has learnt to mistrust Mirabella's plans. Her helper must have been her nephew. No doubt the setting of the murder scene was her work. And that, only when things went wrong, would she have appealed to Michael. And then, while she did a Salome to Samuels's Herod, Michael must have been hidden somewhere near waiting to make the substitute footprint. One sufficiently like the first for the substitution to have a chance of escaping notice."

"Pity the lie of the land didn't permit of our approaching silently," said Engleman bitterly. "It would have given me great pleasure to have caught that young man red-handed. But there, in your opinion, he is probably just another lovable screwball."

Finch's face sobered. "He's quite a formidable young man. Not made any the less so because he has a sense of humour."

When the two men reached Hone Police Station a message was coming in for the Inspector. When he joined Finch in Mrs. Hobday's sitting room, he was jubilant.

"Although it's not being made public," he said, "the Superintendent's dramatic development has taken place. There was a single perfect fingerprint on one of those sling-back shoes belonging to Miss Sumner. It was a queer place to find one, high up on the inside of the heel. That's how the murderer came to miss it. I suppose there are circumstances in which you could pick up a pair of shoes in that fashion. If, for instance, they were lying on their sides. He may have held one up, pretending to admire it."

"He may even have said, 'Charming as they are I don't want to fall over them and break *my* neck.'"

Engleman laughed. "You're making my flesh creep."

Finch looked at him solemnly. "Personally this particular murderer always has made my flesh creep."

The folk dancers had never had such large audiences. Or found their company so much in demand. At first they had found it pleasant, even a little gratifying but this had soon palled. They had taken to going about in groups, adopting a rough, rude, and non-co-operative attitude. When the police had arrived to take everyone's fingerprints, they had become quite disenchanted.

Clare and Antonia, leaving Hone Court for their walk to Treadle Bay, joined one such group. No one recognised them and in Hone they were able to attach themselves to the straggling line of pilgrims toiling up the downs. They even stood with them and stared at the Race Rocks.

It was a wonderfully still day. A haze lay over the sea. The tide was high. They could see only the exposed tips of the rocks and the sinister sluggish movement of the blue grey water.

Antonia felt disgust at the ill informed and sometimes ghoulish comments heard on every side. She was anxious for Clare's sake but although her companion's face had grown pale her expression was so remote that Antonia came to the conclusion that she was scarcely aware of the proximity of other people.

They walked on.

Treadle Bay Cottage was not of much interest to Hone's influx of visitors. Besides it was too far away and too difficult to get to. Clare and Antonia soon found themselves alone. The downs grew empty. There was neither farm nor building in sight. Even the Epps cottage lay farther inland lost in a dip in the hills. The sense of peace and space returned. The lark's song and the murmuring sea became the only sounds to be heard.

They came to the top of a rise and looked down on the loneliness of Treadle Bay.

"And Keith loved it," said Clare wonderingly.

"You never visited him?"

(147)

"No, he often asked me. I never came because of Roger. What would have been the good?"

A tall shambling figure came out of the cottage and made off hurriedly over the downs.

"Tom Epps," Antonia commented surprised. "What on earth was he doing there?"

"I remember Keith writing to me about him. He said then that he suspected Tom of going into the cottage when it was empty. Evidently he was right."

"Then Roger must be out."

Clare had been watching Tom Epps growing smaller and smaller in the distance. "Don't look so troubled, small Antonia. If Tom can get in so can we," she said, smiling for the first time.

The sitting room of the cottage had been plainly but comfortably furnished. It had been made almost luxurious by the addition of articles belonging, Antonia supposed, to Roger. These last included an expensive record player. A rack full of records stood on the mantelpiece.

Over it hung the portrait Clare had made of her brother. It showed the head and shoulders of a plain young man with a thin intelligent face. There was about him such an eager zest for life. So much sweetness and gaiety of expression that Antonia felt the sudden tears prick behind her eyelids.

On the mantelpiece below the portrait lay a bunch of half-dead wild flowers.

Clare touched them with sensitive, lingering fingers. Then suddenly she sank into a tall straight-backed chair, her head bowed over the table. Her body was racked with harsh painful sobs. She struck the tabletop over and over with her clenched fist, writhing in the agony of an unbearable loss.

Antonia crept out of the cottage. She walked down to the edge of the sea, noticing how the mist was thickening. How already it was trailing faint wisps across the valley.

Presently she began to think about Roger's record player. To speculate whether it could be connected with the record at the Thatched Cottage. To wonder whether perhaps the title had been an allusion to Dee and the man who later on had

(148)

murdered her. *Romeo and Juliet*. It might have seemed appropriate at the time.

There was nowhere in Hone where the record could have been bought but in Winstead—? Yes, it might well have come from there. It might even have been purchased in Dee's company. Antonia decided to make her own enquiries taking with her the photographs of Dee which she had collected when she had been expecting to go looking with Michael for news of her.

Clare came out of the cottage. Her violent grief had given place to a look of exhaustion that recalled to Antonia her first appearance at Hone Court.

Under Clare's arm was tucked the portrait of her brother. "I know now that I intended all along to take this," she confided. "I have left Roger a note. He will understand."

Before Antonia could broach the subject of the record Clare added: "I'm going to catch the bus into Winstead now. I'm having tea with George. Why don't you come? He'd be delighted."

They were walking back towards Hone as she spoke.

"I must go back to the cottage," Antonia answered. "Perhaps we can meet later. If so I'll come round to the Grand and look for you."

"You do that, love," Clare agreed cordially.

Outside the Thatched Cottage the group of people had grown. They peered in over the gate and muttered among themselves. Antonia pushed through them.

Some instinct told the crowd that she was not a mere sightseer like themselves. In an unnerving and utter silence she walked, heels clicking, down the garden path.

There was a young pink and white constable now on duty in the cottage. He saw Antonia coming and opened the front door for her. Then he stepped outside and walked deliberately down the path, a portentous frown on his childlike brow, for several of the sightseers had followed the girl through the garden gate.

Left alone in the cottage Antonia hurried across the room to the record player and memorised the details on the label. This done she pulled open one of the bureau's drawers and

took out the photographs of Dee from where she had distract-
edly thrust them.

When the constable returned she was checking the money
in her purse. "If anyone wants me I shall be at the Grand in
Winstead," she told him. "I'm having tea with Mr. Harker and
Miss Vesey."

"Then it's no good my offering you a cuppa? I was just going
to make one."

"No thanks. I must be off. But you'll find a fruit cake on the
tin in the dresser. Do have some and anything else you fancy."

"Thank you, miss." He looked from the window. "Don't
know how you'll get away from that lot. A proper lot of ghouls
they are."

"I shall manage. There is another way out." One she and Dee
had often used when they had seen some boring visitor approaching. Getting in the same way was not as easy but it could
be done.

The constable went into the kitchen. Left alone Antonia
looked about her curiously, glad suddenly that he was in the
next room. She had always understood that, in houses in which
a tragedy had taken place, there remained an impression of the
victim's identity. A mental vision lurking with sad familiarity
in the far corners. There was nothing of that here.

The room, the cottage had grown strange and unfriendly.
Wrapped in a heavyweight of silence, an awful remoteness. As
if, all along it had had an uncaring consciousness that something
terrible was going to happen within its walls.

She went into the kitchen. Said good-bye to the constable
and let herself out of the back door, running quickly across the
lawn and round the end of the beech hedge which separate the
flower garden from what had once been a vegetable garden
and now was a patch of rough grass.

A tool shed stood some few feet from the thick outer hedge.
She climbed on to its roof by way of an ancient garden roller.
She was seen from the gate. A cry of astonishment went up.
Before their astounded gaze she seized a stout branch growing
above her head. Hand over hand she progressed towards the
parent trunk, then dropped to the ground and was lost to sight.

A quick glance around showed her that she had this part of the woods to herself. She drew a deep sigh of relief as she hurried from the vicinity of the cottage. She was climbing over the stile into the main road when she saw Michael coming towards her.

"Hello! Why all this furtive haste?" he asked cheerfully.

"I'm getting away from the sightseers at the cottage."

"By way of the tool-shed roof? That takes me back."

Antonia looked at him suspiciously. "You sound very cheerful."

"That just shows the natural egotism of the human race. The police are taking everyone's fingerprints, which suggests that they have those of the murderer. It suggests further that those prints don't match mine, which they have already." Michael gave her one of his shrewd looks. "You've been going about with the Chief Inspector. Perhaps you know where the fingerprints were found?"

"Going about? You make it sound quite festive." Antonia had, of course, guessed the answer to Michael's question sometime previously.

"So you're not saying. Then may I ask what you have been doing since we last met?"

"I walked with Clare to Treadle Bay Cottage. She wanted the sketch she did of her brother." Antonia added rather uncomfortably, "Roger wasn't there so she took it and left him a note."

"A bit cool, wasn't it?"

"Oh, I don't know," Antonia answered airily. "Anyway Clare caught the bus into Winstead. I'm meeting her there and we are going to have tea with George."

Michael glanced at her quickly. "She hasn't, you know. Gone into Winstead I mean. I walked slap into her not ten minutes ago on the downs."

Antonia stared. "How extraordinary. I suppose she forgot something while we were at the cottage."

"Perhaps she merely wanted to go through Roger's correspondence. She couldn't do *that* while you were there."

"That's a beastly thing to say," said Antonia hotly. "Just because you prefer Mrs. Harker."

Michael's smile vanished. "In an adult sort of way," he said stiffly, "Judith Harker is a very attractive woman."

"Adult is right," said Antonia with an angry laugh. "She is old enough to be your mother."

Michael's good humour returned. "Puss, puss," he remarked grinning. Adding: "Take my advice. Steer clear of the pale Miss Vesey and don't try doing any detective work on your own. It would be an awful waste if you ended up on a mortuary slab."

Threat or genuine concern, Antonia asked herself as, a moment later she climbed into the bus. Michael was still smiling. And what had he got against Clare anyway?

The bus was entering the outskirts of Winstead when his sports car flashed out of the mist and into the town. Antonia had not expected this and found it a little sinister.

Winstead was an old town. It was built on a hill. As Antonia climbed one of its steep streets, she left the mist behind her. She tried a couple of stores where gramophone records were sold but no one could help her. Most of the assistants recognised the snaps of Dee but rather because they had seen photographs of her than that they could remember selling the record.

Plainly they wanted to help but it was still the season. The shops were full of visitors. In the winter they might have remembered but not now.

Antonia crossed the main square and hurried down a narrow street connecting two wider ones. There was no traffic here and the mist was thick. It swallowed up pedestrians. Footsteps too echoed back from the high walls and had an unpleasant way of seeming to be keeping pace with her own.

She emerged thankfully into the main road and went into a music shop. Here she was no more successful in her quest. Coming out she ran into Roger.

"Antonia! Well met. What are you doing here?" He smiled so enchantingly that she found herself smiling delightedly back.

"Oh—just trying to pass the time."

Roger's handsome face twisted in a slight grimace. "Aren't we all? Although at the moment I have a definite objective—and a pretty aggravating one too. Some clot from a garage identified me as the man riding in the car with your friend last Thursday. And, before you shrink from me, let me say that I have a complete alibi. It even satisfied the police—when they got round to going into it. Trouble is that before they'd checked it they impounded my car, took it from the garage in Hone where I keep it. Now they've had the gall to tell me that I could come in and fetch it at any time convenient to me." His handsome face grew thoughtful. "Queer really. The police were full of veiled threats, talk of an identity parade and of hoping to find some trace that Dee Sumner had been in my car. Then suddenly it was all over. I could go."

Said Antonia slowly: "I think they must have found the murderer's fingerprints somewhere because they're busy fingerprinting everyone in Hone."

"So that's why they lost interest. It lets me out—and Michael. The police already had our prints."

Antonia sighed. "But finding the murderer seems farther off than ever," she pointed out.

"How about that sullen-looking brute, Tom Epps?"

"Roger! Who would make an appointment to meet *him* in the woods?"

"True. I'd forgotten that point. I shall have to give it some more thought." He smiled at Antonia. "Tell you what, we will get together some time soon and exchange ideas." He grew serious. "No, I mean it. Someone has got to finish this business. And now I must go and collect my car. D'you happen to know where the police station is?"

"It's miles away," Antonia answered. "At least, it's not really as bad as that. It's in a turning almost opposite the pier."

"Christ!" cried Roger revolted. He rushed away down the hill.

The mist was now billowing in from the sea. It had taken the low lying parts of the town from view and was creeping upwards. Antonia could hear the traffic moving slowly about her. One or two cars passed cautiously, side lights gleaming pale and yellow. Pedestrians were quickly swallowed up.

Anxious about her chances of getting home Antonia decided she had time to try only one more shop. As she hurried along a narrow thoroughfare her eyes were caught by something in a shop window. She stood staring, full of a rising excitement, not unmixed with consternation. There in the window, amid a collection of men's trendy ties, shirts, pullovers, fobs, and watches were some wide silver bracelets in various designs. Men's bracelets—and one of them was exactly like the one she had thought had belonged to Dee.

Or was it?

The details of the bracelet's appearance that had been so clear in her mind two days ago was clear no longer. She decided that, before telling the police she must go back to the cottage and make certain.

As she ran down the hill she paused to look back. For an instant she saw the tall shadowy figure of a man standing looking in at the shop window. It was too foggy for her to decide whether she knew him or not. And even as the thought crossed her mind he was lost to view in the mist.

She hurried on in the direction of the bus stop. Her mind was filled with the implications of her find—if it were a find.

The murderer's bracelet! If it should prove to be that, then it would follow that it was the bracelet he had come searching for that first night. There were other, even more unpleasant implications. Such as the one that having searched everywhere else, he must have stood at the foot of her staircase considering whether he should go up or not. As she was a light sleeper she could guess pretty accurately what would have happened if he had done so.

Only was it the same bracelet? Dee had always had a liking for rather barbaric chunky-looking ones. She had had a large collection of them. Not all expensive but all effective looking. She—

Antonia's thought broke off there. She had just caught sight of Mr. Epps getting into his van. Here was a quick way of getting back to Hone.

Waving and calling his name, Antonia ran towards him.

ELEVEN

The fact that the murderer's finger-prints had been discovered was soon known. A gratified Superintendent Bollard admitted to the press that this was so, but he reiterated that at the moment he couldn't enlarge on the subject. As the afternoon passed and it seemed more and more probable that his quarry had escaped, if only for the time being, he was not so happy.

In Hone the news that the police were taking all male finger-prints caused a sensation. Those who had expressed doubts and cast aspersions in the direction of Sebastian Chant hastened to withdraw them. Or, more brazenly, to deny ever having made them.

Finch, with the discrediting of Craddock's find, had, undeservedly he felt, fallen from favour with the local police. He was motoring slowly back from Hone Police Station when he nearly ran down a woman who stepped suddenly from out of the mist. She was carrying a loaded shopping basket. It was Mrs. Epps and she was full of apologies.

Finch brushed them aside. "Get in and I'll run you home." He stretched out an arm and opened the far door. "Can't have you getting yourself run over."

Her face, under a neat hat, broke into a smile. "That's good of you, sir, but shan't I be taking up your time?"

"That's something of which I have plenty. I seem to be a bit unpopular with the Winstead police."

Mrs. Epps gave a sniff. "They're afraid you'll come up with the solution. That's what it is."

"Did anything come of your enquiries?"

"For Miss Dee and her car? No, sir. No one about here could have seen her or they'd have said so before now."

Finch nodded. "A pity."

After a moment Mrs. Epps remarked: "Mr. Epps had his fingerprints taken. They'd have taken Tom's too but he was scared and ran away. Not that he is frightened of Mr. Hobday. Tom knows him well enough. It's just that he is easily upset."

They came to the gate leading to the downs. Finch got out of the car and opened the door for his passenger. "I'll carry your basket," he offered. Mrs. Epps looked embarrassed. "Unless," he added politely, "you'd rather that I did not."

Mrs. Epps smiled. "It isn't that. It's—well, I was going to whistle for my Tom. Mr. Epps will be wanting his tea and the boy is never where he ought to be."

"If that's all go ahead and whistle."

"It's a bit loud."

"I'm prepared." Finch had expected Mrs. Epps to produce a whistle from her handbag. Instead, she put two fingers in her mouth and let out an ear-splitting sound.

"It has to carry some way," Mrs. Epps remarked apologetically. She caught Finch's eye and burst out laughing. "My Tom may be anywhere. And he hasn't much sense of time."

They walked on towards the cottage.

"There he is," said Mrs. Epps suddenly.

Finch looked in the direction of her pointing finger.

The dark figure of Tom Epps had appeared suddenly striding along the downs, the mist swirling about him. He held his head high. He appeared tall, powerful, and full of purpose. He might, Finch thought, have been one of the early gods bestriding his natural habitat.

"I saw Mr. Frampton like that on the evening of Miss Dee's

disappearance," Mrs. Epps remarked. "That's how I knew he didn't have anything to do with it. Just about half-past six it were. I'd come out to whistle for Tom and there he was—only going the other way towards Treadle Bay along the crest of the downs."

"The local police were quite satisfied with Mr. Frampton's alibi," said Finch. But he was not thinking about Roger. He was aware that he had come to the end of the search. So that's how it happened, he thought. It was as simple as that.

He said good-bye to Mrs. Epps. Reversed his car down the lane and returned to the Hone Police Station.

Engleman had, bad-temperedly, taken possession of Mrs. Hobday's sitting room. He sat there, glumly receiving news of the failure to find anyone whose fingerprints matched the one on the sling-back shoe.

He looked up as Finch entered. "What do you want?" he demanded.

"Eternal friendship," said Finch promptly.

Engleman snarled at him.

Finch pulled up a chair and straddled its seat, his arms resting along its back. "I've solved your mystery for you."

"You have to be joking."

Finch was pained. "Ben, would I joke on such a subject?"

Engleman considered. "From what I know of you, yes."

"Well, put my news another way. Let's say I know where we can find the original of that fingerprint."

Engleman stared. "Where is that?"

"At the morgue in Winstead."

"Now I know you're joking."

"I'm not, Ben. I'll prove it. We'll take McKnight with us and motor into Winstead. Someone can ring up Bollard after we've gone. That way he is bound to be there to meet us."

The morgue was built in the Victorian style. It was ornate in dark red brick, now grimy with age. It had recently reached its centenary but with neither celebration nor rejoicing.

Its stout oak door was opened by the mortuary attendant. He was a thin, sandy-haired man with a morose and furtive air. Superintendent Bollard, he told Engleman, was awaiting their arrival. From his tone of voice it was plain that no joy could be expected from the reunion. He showed them into a large but bleak-looking waiting room.

The Superintendent rose from one of the chairs. Hostility for the Yard man was written all over his broad face. "I got your most extraordinary message." Adding ominously: "I only hope that you are not wasting my time."

Finch looked at him sleepily. "I feel the same," he said in his soft voice. "I don't mind your wasting your time, but I do deprecate it when someone wastes mine." And suddenly he looked a formidable man.

"No offence," said Bollard hastily. And then raising his voice to cover his discomfiture: "Now then! Now then! Let's get on with it, Engleman. Let's get on."

They walked down a wide-tiled passage and into a drab room, cold, smelling of disinfectant and lighted by skylights. Here, McKnight and the mortuary attendant were awaiting them. A covered body had already been wheeled out.

McKnight was eying it almost nervously. "It's not a pretty sight," he said, "but we only need to see his left hand."

"Get on with it, man," cried Bollard. He did not like the place. He did not like the company—either the dead or the living.

McKnight got to work on his rather gruesome task. The big room was very quiet. The atmosphere was tense. It did not take the sergeant long to get the dead man's fingerprints. Nor to compare them with the one found on the shoe. It only seemed long.

Finally McKnight turned to Finch. His face had paled. It bore a strange, almost awed look. "You were right, sir," he said simply. "The print on the shoe was made by the forefinger of Mr. Vesey's left hand. It's almost as if the dead had spoken."

Bollard looked confused. The dead might have spoken to the sergeant. They had left him unenlightened. "D'you mean that Keith Vesey murdered Miss Sumner before he went fishing?" he demanded of Finch. "Then who cleared up in the cottage? And who murdered the second girl? I don't understand."

Engleman was staring straight in front of him. "Come to think of it, who'd leave a girl like Dee to go fishing with a couple of fellows? Damned if I would—or anyone else in his right mind."

Something of the truth came to Bollard. "What d'you say to that, Mr. Finch?" he demanded anxiously.

"I'd say that I'd been wrong," Finch answered, his forehead creased. "I ought to have taken more interest in the Spaniards."

Bollard gave a hollow laugh. "There you have got me foxed," he said, as if everything else were crystal clear.

The telephone rang in the office. The mortuary attendant hurried away. He was soon back. "That was a telephone message for you, sir," he told Bollard. "Miss Vesey and Mr. Harker are at the police station. They're anxious to see you."

Finch nodded. "Perhaps they've looked into the matter of the Spaniards," he murmured in his soft voice. He turned at the door, adding politely: "It's been an interesting ole case— what I've seen of it."

Mr. Epps put Antonia down at the beginning of the lane. "Sure you'll be all right, miss?" he asked dubiously.

"Quite certain," Antonia answered. "I shan't be alone in the cottage. There is a policeman there." Adding in a burst of confidence: "This is going to be my last visit. I don't like the cottage any more." She climbed out of the van, waved a farewell and hurried away.

On each side of the lane shifting mist was gathering. It twisted like a shroud across the fields. Even as she watched the cows lost their legs. The treetops became detached, seeming to float in the air.

Antonia walked faster and a small sliver of mist, like a groping hand slid into the lane and accompanied her on her way.

She walked lightly and warily, not liking the mist. Wondering whether there would still be anyone hanging about the garden gate. There was no one. It all seemed quiet and deserted. So much so that she was conscious of a vague uneasiness.

Her feet rang on the garden path. The mist hung cottage came into view. The front door remained closed. The windows faced her with a lidless stare.

She knocked but no one answered. The truth came to her then. The police guard had been withdrawn. She was alone. Alone with the swirling mist, the silence, and the loneliness.

For a moment she was tempted to abandon her project. Leave the question of the bracelet unsolved. She thought of her dead friend, expecting that the exercise would bolster up her courage. She found, to her consternation that it only made the question of her departure more acceptable.

You'll only be here five minutes, she encouraged herself. Five minutes to get the bracelet, pack your clothes and be off. Nothing can possibly happen in that short time.

She took out her key and with a hand that was not quite steady let herself in. She paused, her back against the closed front door.

"Is any one here?" Her voice very small and hollow-sounding fell on the silence and was swallowed up. There came no answer. The only sound to be heard was her own shallow breathing and the clock ticking away on a high bracket.

Shivering, she crossed the floor and fled up the stairs to her bedroom. There she jerked open one of the small drawers of the dressing table and took out the bracelet. She saw that it was exactly like the one in the shop window in Winstead. She wondered why, when she had seen it before, she had not realised that it was intended for a man's wrist.

She wrapped it in a screw of tissue paper and dropped it into her bag. And now she was seized with a sense of terrible urgency. A desperate need to be gone.

She pulled her suitcase from under the bed. She opened the wardrobe door, taking out the frocks and packing them in feverish haste. Once she paused, tense, listening. There was nothing to hear. She turned her head and looked behind her. The room was just as it had been before, quiet and empty.

She went to the dressing table. She pulled out the drawers one after another, tipping the contents into the suitcase.

(160)

Straightening her back she caught sight of her own reflection in the mirror and paused to stare at it nervously.

She snapped the fastening of her case and shrugged herself into a coat. She picked up her bag. There, that was finished. She looked about her. No, nothing else that she must have. She —and then she froze where she stood.

There had come a sound from down below. The door opening. A movement of the petrified air. Footsteps sensed rather than heard. Antonia's whole being opened itself to the awful realisation of the moment.

The murderer had come for the bracelet.

With a thudding heart Antonia crept to the tiny landing and looked down into the sitting room.

Roger stood at the foot of the stairs smiling up at her. "You're a careless nymph, my small Antonia. You left your keys in the lock," he said. He juggled them for a moment in his hand, then threw them on to the high mantelshelf. He looked at her again. His smile faded. "I have frightened you, silly clot that I am."

Relief had flooded over Antonia. Her spirits rose with a bound. This was Roger, Roger doubly exonerated by the police. The one person who could not be the murderer. "If I had to do a silly thing like leaving the key in the door I was lucky it was you who came along," she declared smiling down at him.

"But you were just going back to Hone Court? Never mind. I'll walk part of the way with you."

"Carrying my suitcase?"

He nodded. "Carrying your suitcase."

Antonia came down the stairs. How different it all looked now that she was no longer alone. "I just want to get a cardboard box. Then we can be off." She found that she was still clutching her bag. She put it down on the oak chest and crossed to the cupboard.

It was a big one built into a recess. In it were stacked all kinds of things. The garden chairs, an elaborate hammock, a croquet set, a model railway someone had once given Dee, tennis racquets and golf clubs. There was a collection of cardboard boxes of all sizes stored on a shelf.

Antonia climbed onto a three-legged stool to get one. "What made you come?"

"I was on my way back to Hone when suddenly a possible solution of the problem we were discussing in Winstead came to me." Roger added in an amused voice, "You still seem on the short side. Better let me get that box. What size had you in mind?"

"Something small—to take some jewellery."

Roger had come into the cupboard as he spoke. Now he stepped close behind her. And with him came that faint expensive scent she had smelt once before. When she had opened another door—on another enclosed space—on another day.

The *murderer!* In spite of all appearances to the contrary this was the murderer. And she had in her bag what he wanted most—the bracelet. Her thoughts raced, Roger's offer to walk with her through the woods now had an awful connotation. Antonia, who had thought upstairs that she had reached the limits of fear, knew now that it had not been so. Her veins ran ice. There was a roaring sound in her head. A slow denigrating horror wrapped her round. She was held motionless by a feeling of utter hopelessness and despair.

Nonetheless, she must have made a movement for the stool overturned. She was thrown to the floor. Something hard struck her ribs. Something sharp clawed at her leg.

"O-oh!" Antonia drew a long shuddering breath and found the sudden shock and pain of her fall had broken the spell of terrified immobility that had gripped her. A sort of cold anger took its place, a desperate resolve. She must think of some way of quitting the cottage. In the mist she might have a chance of getting into the woods and safety over the tool-shed roof.

"Are you all right, Antonia?" Was there an edge of coldness, of suspicion in Roger's voice?

"I—I think so." Only not too all right. "I've twisted my ankle, broken my ribs and given myself concussion." Antonia's voice shook. She hoped Roger would ascribe it to the shock of her fall. If only he would move away. Not stand there, towering over her.

She yearned now to move for another reason. She found that

(162)

this time she had had no difficulty in raising a ghost. A ghost who shared the cupboard with her, flesh still slightly warm to the touch, dark red hair streaming across her breast.

Doubting her ability to stand, Antonia crawled hastily on all fours past Roger's legs and pulled herself up by the couch. She flashed him a quick, tremulous smile. "I really did hurt myself," she said. She bent as if to examine her leg, letting her hair fall over her face shrouding it from view. Why, she wondered, had she not noticed before that his eyes were cold and utterly expressionless? "These tights were new this morning," she complained, "now they're ruined."

"And it looks as if you will have a nice bruise there tomorrow." Roger had emerged from the cupboard. His voice had regained its amiability. "Here's the box I got down for you. What are you going to do with it?"

"Dee had a few pieces of jewellery with her. It doesn't seem very sensible to leave them in an empty cottage," Antonia answered, improvising glibly. "I thought I'd do them up and post them back to London." She felt almost lightheaded at her own resourcefulness. Besides, miraculously, a plan had come into her mind. Not much of a plan but then, as Dr. Johnson had so truly said of the dog that walked on its hind legs, "It is not done well, but you are surprised to find it done at all."

It was the same with her plan.

She opened her handbag and almost cried out. In it were her keys. So that had been a lie. She had not left her keys in the lock. Roger had let himself into the cottage with Dee's keys. They were Dee's keys which he had thrown so carefully out of her sight. Keys taken from her friend after she was dead.

"You look a bit queer. Let me get you a drink?" Mercifully Roger's pleasant voice sounded genuinely anxious.

"You have a drink if you like. I'll make myself some tea in a minute." She picked up the cardboard box and put into it the bracelet, still in its twist of tissue paper. "Tell me, what was the solution you mentioned?"

"It occurred to me that it might have been Keith who came here with your friend. He was in Winstead at about the right time that afternoon and he had come on quite a bit lately. A lot of people seemed to have found him irresistible."

Antonia stared at him incredulously. "What an extraordinary idea." She was not alluding to Roger's suggestion but to something his voice had betrayed to her. It had told her that, far from being Keith's devoted friend, he had hated him. His words she took to be a reaffirmation of his intention to kill her. How else could he have afforded to say them, for he had been telling the truth as he knew it?

She moved past him towards the kitchen. "I'm going to put on the kettle and make some tea," she said. "Then you must tell me about your theory. I must say it sounds rather unlikely."

Now that she could not see Roger her imagination had full rein. In her mind's eye she saw him, not going to look for the bracelet as she had hoped, but staring after her, complacency dying, suspicion taking its place. The temptation to look back and reassure herself was almost irresistible.

Then he spoke. He said—incredibly it seemed to her: "How you girls fly to tea in an emergency. You seem to think it a nostrum for every ill known to mankind."

She did not answer. She could not. Her throat seemed to have closed up. She came to the kitchen door. Blindly she put out a hand and pushed. The door opened. She was in the kitchen and out of Roger's sight.

Hurriedly she ran the cold water. Rattled the kettle on the stove. Then she was at the back door stealthily turning the key. The door opened and she slipped out into the garden.

For a moment she saw it ghostly and unfamiliar in the mist. The path, the rose bed beyond, some shrubs—and then nothing. A car came slowly along the main road. It passed the end of the lane and went on towards Hone. In imagination she saw it go through the village. Stop before a pleasant-looking house. Saw wife and children run out to greet the driver, all blissfully ordinary—and safe.

She fell on her knees and drew herself on her stomach into the narrow space between a thick shrub and the cottage wall. She lay there, listening.

She heard footsteps in the kitchen. "Antonia?" There was

more enquiry than alarm in the voice. He came to the back door. "Antonia, what's going on?"

Again he stood silent, so near to her that she could have put out a hand and caught him round the ankle. Then he said —addressing himself, as she had hoped he would, to the group of mist-shrouded shrubs: "So you've rumbled me. Mirabella always said you had all your wits about you." He spoke quite pleasantly. "Well, it doesn't matter. There's no way out of the garden except by the gate and I fastened that up when I came in. I'll just make certain it's quite secure, then I'll come and look for you. It should be quite amusing—particularly when I find you."

He moved away not a moment too soon as far as Antonia was concerned. Her teeth had begun to chatter. Her whole body shook in strong recurrent spasms. She heard his footfalls light, unhurried, dwindling away into silence. Now there was nothing to hear but another car going in the direction of Hone. Nothing to see but the strange and indistinct shapes of once-familiar things.

She wondered suddenly whether Roger was indeed walking all the way to the gate. Or whether he was standing still just out of sight, waiting for her to make some betraying move.

She put her ear to the ground. And, miraculously it seemed, very far off, a reverberation rather than an actual sound, she became aware of his retreating steps.

She began to wriggle out from under the bush. Very cautiously she did it. Dragged herself to her feet. Stood straining her eyes, fearful that he might do the impossible. Return in absolute silence. Appear suddenly in front of her—

She set out in a sort of crouching run across the lawn. Heard Roger give a kind of grunt of satisfaction as he turned back. By then Antonia had reached the shelter of the clump of shrubs. She dodged round the end of the beech hedge—and ran straight into someone on the farther side. An arm gripped her. A hand closed over her mouth.

For a moment she thought that it must be Roger. That her nightmare fear had become a reality. Then, raising her agonised eyes, she saw that it was Michael who held her.

(165)

Michael, looking his usual self-possessed and nonchalant self. He smiled at her. Removed his hand, peered closer and grinned broadly.

For the first time Antonia became aware of tangled hair, torn clothes, and mud-stained face. She felt indignant. This was no time for noticing such things. Yet the very naturalness of his reaction brought an obscure comfort with it.

They could hear Roger's approaching footsteps. Michael stepped a little way from Antonia. He engaged in a pantomime show of shadow boxing. Then he pointed to her and then towards the tool shed.

Michael wished her to leave while he fought off Roger? She nodded vigorously, more to show that she understood than because she had any idea of doing so. She had ideas of her own on the subject. They included a carving knife fetched from the kitchen and some screams for help analogous to the whistle of a steam engine.

She did not doubt Michael's strength and skill. It was merely that her experience had left her thinking of Roger as irresistibly malignant and powerful. And suddenly there he was, standing quite still, staring at Michael. Then before either of them could move there came a totally unexpected interruption.

Someone rattled the garden gate. "Drat it! What's got into the thing?" Mr. Epps's voice came, gloriously incongruous to Antonia's ears. A moment later a car turned into the lane.

Roger's face changed colour. He gazed rather wildly about him as if seeking some way of escape. Antonia realised exultantly that he was frightened. That, even as she watched, the fight was going out of him. He turned, racing for the garden gate.

The car stopped. The gate rattled. Mr. Epps's voice was raised in astonished and angry expostulation. There came a pause—of blessed peace it seemed to Antonia. It was broken by a savage and triumphant roar.

"You bastard! I'll kill you," it said.

"Sounds as if George has got him," said Michael cheerfully. And then in a completely different tone of voice: "Don't cry, my small and grubby sweetheart. It's all over now."

TWELVE

That evening Tom Epps was encouraged to tell his story to an audience that included Finch and Hobday. The story that his mother in all innocence had suppressed.

He told how he had seen Roger on the night after Keith's death, shouting in triumph and laughing aloud as he ran exultantly over the downs. "A right Spaniard he was," Tom declared fiercely, remembering Keith Vesey whom he had looked on as a friend.

When he saw that his mother was in tears he was filled with remorse. He assured her that he would never, never repeat his story again. He was more bewildered than consoled when she kissed him lovingly, declaring him to be the best of sons.

Tom's spirits were only restored when Sebastian declared his intention of taking him into Winstead the following morning and buying him anything he fancied. It was an offer that ordinarily would have filled Mrs. Epps with foreboding. Now she only smiled and nodded.

Antonia was little the worse for her experience at the Thatched Cottage. It was Clare who collapsed.

Mirabella, viewing this monumental display of grief with the eye of a connoisseur, took her visitor back to her heart. Clare found herself clasped in two soft arms, their tears mingling and dripping on to a plump bosom.

The Chants' doctor was sent for. Clare was given a sedative and put to bed. Several times during the night Mirabella pattered into the room to brood over her sleeping form. When Clare did awake next morning her hostess' pugface, wearing an expression half anxious, wholly benevolent, was the one she saw.

"What a spectacle I made of myself," Clare muttered, starting up in bed. "And such a self-centred guest as I have been. But I couldn't think of anything but my need for revenge."

"Then you knew that Roger had been responsible for your brother's death?"

"I felt certain of it. And when I stood looking at the Race Rocks with Antonia I realised how easy it would have been to push anyone over the cliffs. I knew then that that was what Roger had done to Keith."

"Lie down again and rest." Mirabella drew the bedclothes up over Clare's shoulders. "I'll send Antonia up with your breakfast. Mr. Finch is coming to luncheon and I expect you'll want to be there."

So, at twelve o'clock Clare was getting up. Antonia sat watching her dress. Clare broke the companionable silence. "Would you mind if I took up with George?"

"Of course not. He isn't the kind of man to mourn Dee for long. Particularly now that there is nothing to be gained. Only" —Antonia looked rather shyly at the older girl—"I think he would be rather an insensitive lover, always expecting you to be on top of your form. Dee was never ill and Mrs. Harker looks as strong as a horse."

"Actually I'm as strong as a horse too but George isn't going to know that." Clare was brushing her long pale hair as she spoke. "I'm going to be much more demanding than either Dee or Judith Harker. In a way I shall have to be. Your friend had money. Mrs. Harker had family, both of which would have impressed George. I shall have to set an artificial value on myself, otherwise he will trample on me."

"It doesn't sound very comfortable," said Antonia doubtfully. She thought how much nicer life with Michael would be.

Clare turned her head, parting her long pale hair, to smile at her companion. "I have a devious nature. I shall enjoy it. It will be like a game with elaborate and intricate rules drawn up by myself."

She piled her hair deftly on the top of her head. "Intense emotion plays havoc with one's looks," she remarked, peering into the mirror. She walked over to the window and stood looking out so dreamily that when she spoke her actual words came as a shock to Antonia.

"It is a most lovely day. I am glad of that. Everyone will be able to enjoy it except Roger. Oh, it's terrible to hate anyone as I hate him." She was silent a moment. Then she said: "I think I knew as soon as I saw the Chief Inspector that Keith's death was going to be avenged. His being here was Fate, Kismet, *Che será será.*"

"If you don't hurry," Antonia rejoined matter of factly, "you'll be late and miss part of what he has to say."

They went downstairs together.

Mirabella had gone about the house all the morning like a small rocket. Except when she thought of Keith, that lively and lovely spirit, she was happy. Sebastian was chastened but safe. Michael had expressed his determination to marry Antonia. This had pleased Mirabella so much, that, on the spur of the moment, she had offered to save the remains of the estate for him. She was relieved when he refused the offer.

She had had a great deal to do. Most of the dancers were leaving that day. The order for milk and eggs must be cancelled once more. The jumbo filled again with unwanted or mislaid articles. Lists must be made. Letters written. Small loans advanced. Transport laid on for those without cars. The sitting room must be filled with flowers and luncheon prepared. Nothing she felt was too good for their expected guest.

When Finch arrived at Hone Court it was a cheerful Michael who opened the front door to him. He was shown into the sitting room where Sebastian stood with his back to the fireplace and an untidy pile of newspapers on the rug at his feet. Judith Harker, with no particular expression on her face, lounged gracefully in a low armchair, a glass in her hand.

Sebastian hurried forward: "My dear fella! Come in, come in. You have met Mrs. Harker."

Judith extended her hand. "We met just in the nick of time. When Superintendent Bollard was thinking of arresting me."

"He nearly arrested me," Sebastian declared. "And now he *has* arrested Roger—although why Roger should have pushed Keith off the cliffs I don't know. And, as far as I can see, the newspapers don't know either. I mean—Keith and Roger were like brothers. David and Jonathan and all that."

"It seems they were more like David and Saul," said Finch dryly. "Didn't he try and pin David to the wall with a javelin? And for no other reason than that he feared that David was going to usurp his position."

Sebastian stared. "Roger jealous of Keith? That can't be right. He has everything—money, charm, good looks, brains. It doesn't make sense."

"Although neither of us realised it at the time," said Finch, "your wife presented me with the answer to that problem when we first met. She described Mr. Vesey as a late developer with a potential for greatness—and Mr. Frampton was not accustomed to rivalry, least of all from Keith Vesey whom he had overshadowed all his life."

"What interests me," said Michael, as he supplied Finch with a drink, "is how you came up with the idea that the mysterious fingerprint belonged to poor old Keith? I mean—it wasn't exactly the most obvious solution."

"It was Mrs. Epps," Finch answered. "She told me that she had seen Roger Frampton walking back to Treadle Bay along the crest of the downs at six-thirty on the Thursday evening. It was misty. The figure she saw was some distance away. And neither the time nor the place fitted.

"How d'you make that out?" Michael asked.

"The time?" Finch answered. "Mr. Frampton had told me that at half-past six that evening you and he were having a drink in the Bull's Head. The place? Well, to get to Treadle

Bay from the village one would walk along the cliff edge. It was only when coming from the vicinity of Hone Court that one would pass within sight of the Epps cottage."

"That's clever." Sebastian was impressed. "And so if it were neither Michael nor Roger making for Treadle Bay then it was probably Keith."

Finch nodded. "And after all, we only had Roger Frampton's word for it that Mr. Vesey had gone fishing."

Mirabella and the girls came in. They greeted Finch as if he had been an old friend.

"Have we missed anything?" Mirabella asked.

Sebastian repeated what Finch had told them.

Mirabella's face clouded over at the mention of Keith's name, but she said only: "Come in to luncheon. And we'll leave any discussion of this tragic affair until afterwards."

As they passed through the doorway she asked: "Have you made any plans yet, Judith?"

"I find life in England too exciting," Judith answered. "I am going back to Southern Ireland to live." She gave a sardonic laugh. "Who knows? In a country where the English are always wrong I may even find myself something of a heroine."

The meal passed pleasantly enough. A mild euphoria had seized on them all. It faded swiftly when they were back in the sitting room. Now there was tension in the air.

Clare said at once: "I want to hear everything, please. What you found out. What Roger said—most of all I want to hear what Roger said."

Sebastian was fussing with the coffee percolator. "And I hope there's going to be none of that *sub judice* nonsense," he said in a disgruntled voice.

"Superintendent Bollard gave me permission to tell you what we know," Finch answered with conscious virtue. "He even gave me a copy of Roger Frampton's statement, though I must warn you that it isn't going to be pleasant to hear."

"I want to hear it," Clare said firmly. "It's only by knowing everything that I shall be able to put it behind me."

"I want to hear it too," Antonia agreed, although she was not at all certain that she did.

(171)

Sebastian had turned staring at Finch. Now he said: "D'you mean that Roger has confessed to the murders?"

"Only because something came to light that made it useless for him to do anything else. And I must admit I got the impression that he enjoyed giving an account of what he had done. Like most criminals he is convinced of his own cleverness and that only bad luck led to his arrest. And here I'd like to say that, for the sake of continuity and if no one objects, I will allude to the principals in the case by their first names—as Roger does."

No one objected so Finch began by dealing with a couple of minor points, the first of which had little influence on the case.

"The police in Winstead," he said in his small voice that yet carried to every corner of the room, "were more successful than Antonia. They found the shop where Keith had bought the record, the presence of which in the Thatched Cottage had so puzzled her." At this the girl looked abashed and Sebastian wagged a reproving head at her. "He was alone when he bought it. The police also found the shoes Roger wore when he threw the dogs off the scent by wading down the stream."

"How did they manage that?" Michael asked.

"You must ask your uncle," Finch answered.

Sebastian chuckled, pleased with this part of the affair.

"It was during my shopping expedition with Tom Epps. He had set his heart on looking like the most trendy of visitors. We bought frilled shirts in startling colours, jeans and a ghastly pair of white and blue canvas shoes. It was these shoes that reminded Tom that he had seen Roger, late Saturday night, push a pair of shoes down an old rabbit burrow. Not that Tom saw anything significant in this. It was simply that one pair of shoes reminded him of another pair."

Finch nodded. "Hobday retrieved them and they are now at the forensic laboratory."

"It's odd how Tom Epps keeps coming into the picture," Antonia commented. "I mean he's not the most brilliant brain about here."

"All the same it was Tom I went looking for yesterday afternoon," said Clare. "Seeing him coming out of Treadle Bay Cottage and later finding those wild flowers on the mantelpiece under Keith's portrait made me wonder whether he knew anything about my brother's death. I found him on the downs and he told me how happy Roger had been after Keith's death. It seems that Tom was in the habit of watching for my brother's return to Treadle Bay. If he were alone Tom would go down and join him. On Thursday evening Keith didn't come at all and Tom, sensing that something was wrong, set himself to watch." She smiled faintly. "There isn't much more to say. When I went into Winstead I told—" She paused slightly, remembering Judith's presence. Then she quietly substituted the more formal mode of address. "I told Mr. Harker Tom's story and he advised me to go to the police."

"Very sensible advice," said Finch. He wondered how far Judith had been deceived by Clare's substitution of one name by another. Or indeed, whether she was meant to be deceived. There was something rather feline about Clare's dealings with her fellow men—or women.

"But unnecessary," said Clare. "As soon as I heard that you were here I knew that Keith's death would be avenged."

Finch nodded. "Yes, you were lucky there," he said quite seriously. "Although, mind you, no one could have proved that Roger had been responsible for Keith's death. It was the perfect murder." He drew some papers from his pocket and unfolded them. "Roger's statement begins with a comment on the relationship of these two young men as seen by one of them. I'll read it to you." He did so. "It was as if one of those ghastly little paperbacks on how to think yourself into success had actually worked. I had always assured Keith that he could be a great success. And suddenly, damn me, if he didn't begin to be one."

Clare nodded. "It was after they went up to Oxford that Roger began to be jealous of my young brother. There they were accepted into an intellectual circle. That and the freedom from petty restrictions was exactly what Keith needed. He began to expand. To attract people. And Roger resented it

(173)

bitterly. He never said anything but I have seen him look at Keith—" She shivered, her face pale.

"Oh dear!" cried Mirabella distressed. "And I was always praising Keith to Roger. The originality of his mind. His gentle charm—"

"I don't think you need blame yourself. I am sure that Miss Vesey is right. Roger had begun to resent Keith long before they came down here." Finch turned a page. "We come now to that fatal Thursday. The two young men passed the morning in study as was usual, quite unaware that before nightfall one of them would be dead and the other a murderer. Then after an early lunch Keith set out to walk into Winstead where, unknown to Roger, he bought the recording of Tchaikovsky's *Romeo and Juliet*. Roger, meanwhile, had gone into Hone to spend the afternoon with some friends he had made among the visitors. Later this was to afford him a very useful alibi.

"When Roger returned to Treadle Bay at about a quarter to seven he was surprised to find Keith there. He had not gone fishing he told him because in Winstead he had met the most wonderful girl in the world. Before he had even said the name of Dee Sumner, Roger had guessed it. And it seemed to him to be the greatest injury Keith had as yet inflicted on him, for he had been so certain of becoming Dee's lover in private and her escort in public.

"Keith explained how he had been waiting in the square for the lights to change so that he could cross when this fabulous-looking blonde had driven up in an old car. Their eyes had met and in that one instant they had known that they were destined for each other. They had spent a blissful afternoon at the Thatched Cottage just talking—about themselves—about their past and about their future together. Keith explained that he had returned to Treadle Bay only to pick up his toothbrush and razor and to say good-bye to Roger.

"Still unaware of his companion's seething resentment he talked of his lady love's charms. He repeated practically everything they had said to each other. Such as Dee's determination to love the classics for his sake. And his to cultivate a taste for pop."

"Oh dear!" said Mirabella, wiping her eyes. "It—it sounds so innocent—like the Garden of Eden."

"It sounded nauseating rubbish to Roger," Finch commented dryly. "In fact he had soon had enough of it. He invented an appointment in Hone and, tragically for himself, Keith decided that he would walk part of the way with him.

" 'We walked up over the downs. The mist was patchy and not too thick. It lifted suddenly and we saw that there was a boat overturned close to the Race Rocks.' " Finch was reading again from Roger's statement. " 'The bright blue and white of the hull was unmistakable. Keith blamed himself of course. He was a great one for that. He went right to the edge of the cliffs —and that was when I got the idea of giving him a shove. It was a sort of poetic justice. Originally Claud and David had been my friends. But since they seemed to prefer Keith, they could have him.' "

A horrified silence fell on the room. Sebastian broke it.

"It just shows you can never really know anyone," he declared sadly, "not to *know*."

"With Keith's death, as I have said, Roger had committed the perfect crime. Unfortunately for him he could not stop there. Dee knew that Keith had not gone fishing. Furthermore she was expecting him to return by half-past seven and time was running out. Roger's statement goes on 'I had to hurry. I didn't want the girl to get impatient and go to the end of the lane where she could have been recognised. I had no time to provide myself with gloves. This led me on the Saturday evening when things began to get dicey, to get myself invited into the Thatched Cottage. So that, in the unlikely event of my fingerprints being found there, no suspicion would be aroused. As it turned out that muscle-bound fool, George Harker, was there first. He said he wanted to see Dee and that was a laugh. Of course I could easily have persuaded Antonia to let me in but Harker's company was too high a price to pay and there was always tomorrow or so I thought. I was unlucky there, but I didn't worry.

" 'But to get back to Thursday evening. I reached the Thatched Cottage without being seen. Dee opened the front door before I could even knock. I was Roger, wasn't I? Where was Keith? What was wrong? She looked marvellous but it was obvious that Keith had loused up *that* situation as far as I was concerned. So, as she turned to close the front door behind me, I hit her. And a bloody good job I made of it. I took her keys since I planned to come back later. I carried her body out to the car and put it in the boot. It was a bit risky since it wasn't really dark and the mist was thinning but I didn't want her stiffening up on me. Then I went back to the Bull's Head to dinner. I felt wonderful. Almost as if I had been born again.'"

"The beast!" cried Antonia. "The—devil!" Then she burst into tears and Michael took the opportunity to put his arms round her and kiss her.

"I did warn you that it wouldn't be pleasant," said Finch mildly.

"And I s-still want to hear," Antonia declared hiccupping and wiping her eyes with the handkerchief Michael proffered.

"How Roger went back and cleared up we know already," said Finch. "And how the absence of fingerprints in the sitting room presented the police with one of the case's most curious features. For if it was the man who had arrived at the cottage with Dee who had cleaned up why hadn't he remembered what things he had touched? And if it were a second man calling after the first had left, how did he know that the first visitor had been neither upstairs to the bedroom nor out to the kitchen? Once we realised that Keith had been the first man and Roger the second the puzzle was solved.

"We know that everything went well for Roger until the Saturday evening. With Miss Vesey's arrival he recognised that she suspected him of being responsible for her brother's death so he went at once into his rejected lover routine."

"I did try not to show my horror of him," said Clare. "I wasn't very successful because even to be near him filled me with nausea. This he seemed to find amusing. Oh, he was clever, pretending that he loved me—"

"I've been puzzled by that," said Antonia, her voice still a bit shaky. "What g-good did it do him?"

"It made it seem even less likely that he would have done

anything to hurt my brother," explained Clare wearily. "It also would have been an explanation of sorts if I seemed to dislike him or made any accusations. Women turn so many faces to an unwanted lover, from indifference to downright cruelty."

Sebastian nodded. "That's true. I noticed it. Poor devil I said to myself. Clare doesn't care a hoot for him—and he feels it." He looked at Finch. "But carry on, I didn't mean to interrupt."

Finch did so. "To Roger's way of thinking that evening held even greater dangers than those posed by Miss Vesey. Beatrice spoke of seeing things in the mist not meant to be seen and Miss Hughes described a bracelet—silver, chunky and with a defective fastening—which both Roger and Beatrice recognised as having belonged to Keith. That night Roger visited the cottage in an unsuccessful attempt to retrieve the bracelet and next morning Miss Hughes discovered proof that her friend had arrived at the cottage after all."

"But before this happened Beatrice Lynham had telephoned Roger. She told him that early on the Thursday evening she had thought she had seen Keith on the downs. That, at the time, she had believed herself mistaken. But that she now knew, not only that it had been Keith but that he must have been with Dee at the Thatched Cottage since his bracelet had been found there by Miss Hughes—"

"Oh no!" Antonia cried. And then: "So it was my fault Beatrice was murdered."

"Nonsense," said Mirabella stoutly. "Beatrice brought it on herself. She should have gone straight to the police with her story. Not tried to—well, blackmail Roger, as I suppose she did."

"Yes, she wanted a lump sum of five thousand pounds," said Finch with a faint smile. "Or, if that would leave Roger with a feeling of insecurity, he could marry her, for after all, as she pointed out, a wife could not be compelled to testify against her husband."

Sebastian's pink face had paled and Mirabella's had flushed. "The nasty heartless gairl," she cried.

"She paid for her stupidity," Judith pointed out.

"It was a horrible way to die," said Antonia with a shudder. "What did Roger say about it?" Michael asked.

"His only comment was that he realised that she would have to be put away. 'For the sake of appearances'"—Finch was reading again—"'I blustered and pleaded a bit. Then, with a fine show of reluctance I agreed to meet her to talk things over in the lounge of the Bull's Head that afternoon. I knew the silly bitch would take the path through the woods so I hid behind a tree, and as she drew near, I stepped out and twisted her necklace tightly round her throat. It was almost ludicrous to see the look of astonishment and terror on her face.' But to get back to the Monday morning. Beatrice's telephone call had been followed by Roger having to take Clare with him to Winstead when he went to identify David's body. Not that he had minded. He had been amused by her attempts to get some sort of admission out of him.

"In Winstead they had run into George Harker and Roger had realised that Clare intended to enlist his help. He had not liked this but only because he recognised the power given by George's wealth. However his self-confidence remained unshaken. Indeed, right up to the moment of truth in the mist-hung garden of the Thatched Cottage, he had seen himself as inventive, invincible, always one step ahead of anyone else.

"On his return from Winstead he had been told how the word Vesuvian had been found in Dee's writing on the kitchen table, proving that she had been in the cottage. This oversight on his part had annoyed him at first. Later he had found it amusing to see everyone so astonished and bewildered. The fact that one of the party was a well-known police officer only added to the piquancy of the moment.

"Roger had realised that as soon as darkness fell he would have to find a new hiding place for the car and its dead owner. As it fell out he had to wait so long for the police to arrive to question him about Beatrice and her friendship with Keith, that it had been nearly ten o'clock before he had been able to leave Treadle Bay Cottage. He had taken the Bug into the woods, easily evading Sebastian and as we know throwing the police dogs off the scent by walking down the stream to the

(178)

road, where he had concealed one of the many bicycles from Hone Court.

"Next day the garage hand had mistakenly identified him as the man seen with Dee Sumner in her car. When Roger had met Antonia in Winstead he had not been at all worried to hear that the police had found the murderer's fingerprints. The last place he thought in which they would look for their counterpart would be the mortuary. No, he'd seen their meeting simply as indicating an ideal opportunity for him to retrieve Keith's bracelet. And if the police hadn't delayed him so long before letting him take his car he would have found it and been gone long before Antonia's return. As it was he had let himself into the cottage and had been halfway across the room before he had realised that he was not alone. That someone was upstairs in the bedroom.

"*He* realised? What about me?" Antonia demanded. "I nearly died of fright." She added speaking to Finch: "I heard several cars pass while I was hiding from Roger in the garden and I hoped so much that one of them would turn into the lane. What made you come?"

"They came," said Sebastian, "because Michael had the good sense to ring up the police after he had looked into a certain shop window to see what had interested you and sent you hurrying down the hill."

His rebuke passed Antonia by. "So someone *was* following me about," she exclaimed, turning happily to Michael. "It was you."

"I mistrusted that air of sturdy determination I noticed when we met by the stile," Michael answered, grinning. "I'd have reached you before Roger only in my haste I managed to run my car off the road into the ditch. I had to foot it the last half mile. I may add that my speed increased considerably after Roger's car passed me. When I got to the cottage and found the gate tied up I knew that he was there, even though I couldn't see his car, which the police discovered later, he had driven into the garage. I nipped round and in by way of the garden shed. I was sneaking across the grass hoping to take him by surprise when you ran smack into me."

(179)

Antonia shivered involuntarily. "You frightened me so much. I thought it was Roger."

"You were extremely lucky that so many people were so concerned for your safety," said Sebastian. "Michael, Mr. Finch, poor old Epps remembering suddenly that he had heard that the police constable had been withdrawn."

"*Dear* Mr. Epps." Antonia added ruefully, "I can see I didn't behave very sensibly going into the cottage and I'm sorry."

"Wasn't Mr. Finch keeping some special disclosure to the last?" asked Judith in a bored tone of voice.

"So I was," Finch agreed amiably. "It was this. Before Beatrice met Roger she wrote and posted a letter. In it she spoke of seeing Keith, of the bracelet, of her own action in blackmailing Roger and that she was to meet him that afternoon at the Bull's Head."

"So that's what she was doing that afternoon when she wouldn't come out with me," cried Sebastian.

Finch nodded. "She meant to explain to Roger about the letter and so deter him from any thought of doing to her what she suspected him of doing to both Dee and Keith. Unfortunately, as we know, she never had the chance to tell him anything."

"Yes—but who did she write to?" Mirabella asked.

"She addressed the envelope to herself at her home in London. There it was found by the police when, at Superintendent Bollard's request, they went to search her bedroom."

Judith Harker rose to her feet. "How interesting this has been. Quite a revelation. Thank you all so much." She looked Clare up and down and gave a short laugh. "I wouldn't be surprised if George hasn't met his match at last."

"What the devil did she mean by that?" Sebastian demanded when Judith had left the house.

"What indeed?" Mirabella echoed mendaciously. "Really Judith's conversation gets more incomprehensible every day. And every day I get more convinced that Ireland is just the place for her."

"If no one minds I think I'll lie down for a while," said

Clare. She smiled palely at Finch. "Thank you for taking me at my word—and for catching Roger for me."

"Surely it was Mr. Harker who did that," said Finch with his slow smile. "It took three of us to prise them apart."

Clare's smile widened. Now she really looked amused. "Dear George—so masterful—and so determined to lay violent hands on Roger."

"Yes, he is still as hoarse as a crow. He had to write his own statement. He couldn't speak it."

"I'm glad," said Clare. She smiled around her and left the room as quietly and composedly as she had entered it.

"Now I get it," said Sebastian grinning. "George is attracted to Clare—and she, I suspect, is attracted to George's money."

"It will do George a lot of good to know Clare," Mirabella declared briskly.

"But I thought you didn't like her," Sebastian protested. "I thought you and Michael had decided that she was up to something."

"Yes but now we know that that something was to get Roger arrested we quite approve," Mirabella pointed out triumphantly. "Poor girl, there she was shut up in a world of her own. Alone in her agony."

"Alone except for poor George," Michael remarked sotto voce.

Mirabella's smile widened. "Except for poor George," she agreed.

"It seems to me," said Sebastian, staring pointedly at Antonia, "that there is a general pairing up around here."

To Antonia's annoyance she felt her face colouring.

"I like to see a girl blush," said Sebastian approvingly.

"I'd like to see Aunt Mirabella dance again," said Michael hurriedly to cover Antonia's confusion.

Sebastian broke into a roar of laughter. "The Dying Swan? So should I. Mr. Finch, I envy you that."

"I wouldn't have missed it for anything," Finch admitted chuckling.

"I don't see why you should all laugh," Mirabella protested. "I couldn't have been all that unlike Pavlova. I remember a critic writing of her that she showed grace, sensual charm—*and a sense of humour.*"

"I think," said Finch solemnly, "that I prefer the criticism of a French writer. *La danse de toujours—dansée comme jamais.*"

"The dance of everyday," Mirabella translated, "as it was never danced before." She laughed delightedly. "Mr. Finch, I think you are a very rude man."